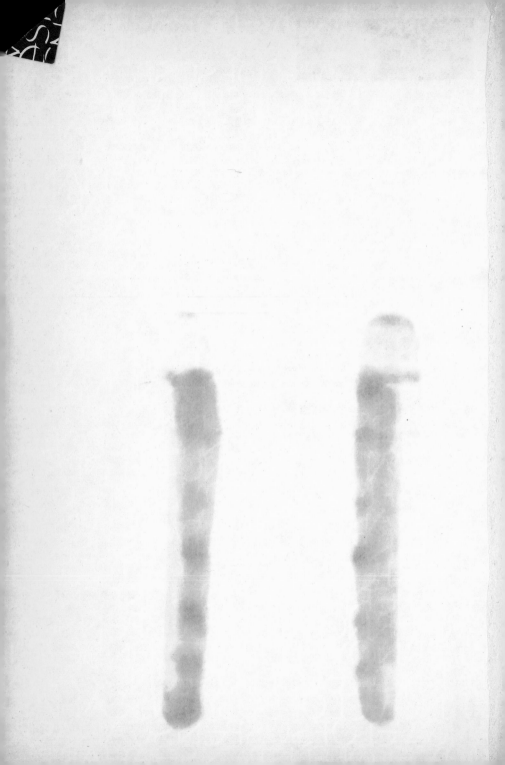

PURLOINING
TINY

A JOAN KAHN BOOK

PURLOINING TINY

TINY

JOHN FRANKLIN BARDIN

HARPER & ROW, PUBLISHERS

New York, Hagerstown, San Francisco, London

A HARPER NOVEL OF SUSPENSE

FIRST EDITION

Designed by Stephanie Krasnow

Library of Congress Cataloging in Publication Data

Bardin, John Franklin.
  Purloining Tiny.
   I. Title
PZ3.B23615Pu   [PS3503.A56374]   813'.5'4   77–10192
ISBN 0–06–010227–6

78 79 80 81 82 10 9 8 7 6 5 4 3 2 1

To Clark

1

INTRODUCING TINY

The presence was there. *He* was behind her. She knew he couldn't be—not here, at this time, or any time any more, in this place or any place. But she knew, even so, that he was behind her.

She must be very calm.

"Why can't you just leave?"

"The act?"

"If that's what you need to leave."

"I couldn't."

"Why? It's not the money?"

"No. It's because then . . . then I'd be alone." Alone with him. He was closer now. She could feel his presence. It was about to happen again; she was afraid this time it would happen, happen all the way, as it never had before. Or had it? Once, many times?

"Is it because you're an orphan?"

"And my mother an alcoholic? And a prostitute? No, I wasn't an orphan." She tried to speak, to tell her doctor about him, about why she was deathly afraid. Her lips trembled. Her body was shaken by a convulsive chill.

She began to weep. But she knew that she must face him out. She must turn about . . . see.

There was no one there. Only the doctor, sitting behind his desk, notebook in hand and silver pencil poised, saying, "Tiny, I'm afraid your time is up."

She walked out of the brownstone building in the East Fifties where the doctor kept his suite of offices, out into the bright sunshine of early June. A nursemaid was walking twins in a perambulator. A young man with blond silky hair and a long wispy mustache walked past her, hands in his pockets, whistling. A woman was trying to park her car in a place too small for it.

Everything seemed so normal. Everything was normal. She had to get hold of herself; she must. She decided to do what she had done so many times before: go to that kinky bar on Madison Avenue. It was absurd, it was bizarre, but the bartender was nice to her.

It was called Once Over Lightly. She went through the outside door and past the checkroom into the cool interior and sat on a barber's chair. There were nine of them lined up beside the bar, and the mirrored back bar had bottles arranged like the accouterments of an old-fashioned tonsorial parlor, though the tall swirly bottles contained not Lilac Vegetal or witch hazel, but such things as lime juice and bitters.

Her eyes were still red and her platinum-blond hair showed where she must have raked it with her hands. She reached in her purse and found a pack of cigarettes. Only one left; she always smoked like a fiend in the psychiatrist's consulting room.

And she couldn't stop weeping—or find her handkerchief.

"It isn't the end of the world, miss." The nice bartender

handed her a cocktail napkin, and she dabbed at her eyes. He had a dark, sober face that crinkled into a handsome smile. She asked for a Scotch with a twist and water on the side.

Her hands trembled so much she dropped her last cigarette on the floor. She wasn't sure she could manage to lift the glass to her lips.

At least he wouldn't come in here. She would be safe here. Oh, this was such nonsense! She had to get hold of herself.

She thought of going back to the doctor, but she knew he had other appointments. She would have to calm herself down. Why, she didn't even know *why* she was afraid of him, or who he was.

She didn't spill her drink and the first sips helped. She dabbed at her eyes with the napkin and looked up at the bartender to thank him, but he was talking to a middle-aged man who had come in and sat in the barber's chair beside hers. He was drinking a highball and he had an open pack of cigarettes on the bar. She had to have a cigarette, had to talk to someone. She decided to be bold.

"Might I have one of your cigarettes?"

"Of course." He offered her the pack and lighted her cigarette. "It takes a while," he said. He had a resonant voice and a fatherly manner.

"What takes a while?"

"Troubles. I've had them."

"How do you know I'm troubled?"

"I don't like to see a woman weep. I don't mean to be presumptuous, but might it help . . ."

"If I talked to you about my troubles? No, I don't think so."

She had some more of her drink and looked straight ahead of her at the bartender, who seemed amused. Well, she needed somebody to talk to, even a stranger. "You could talk to me about yours," she said, still not looking at him.

"It was a long time ago—many years. I broke up with my wife."

"Not uncommon."

"It happens to a lot of us. I know how long it took for me to get used to the fact that she was gone. It's like becoming a widow, or a widower. First I didn't accept that she had really, irrevocably left. Then I shook my fist at God and cried, 'Why did this have to happen to me?' Then a period of mourning set in; for a couple of years I couldn't look at a pretty face like yours. But that passes. What's your name?"

"Tiny."

"You know, you look rather like her. Or it may be an illusion of mine."

"That's a compliment." She realized that she didn't fear the presence any longer.

"Mine's Harry." He nodded at the bartender. "That's Nick."

"He's very nice; I've been coming in and crying on his shoulder for weeks."

"Nick is fine. May I show you her picture?"

"You don't carry it after all those years!"

"I guess it's silly of me."

"I think it's touching."

"May I?"

"Yes, if you'd like."

Harry reached into his pocket and took out his wallet. From it he withdrew a newspaper clipping, yellowed with age. He examined it. He shook his head, then looked at Tiny. The clipping fell from his hand onto the floor. He picked it up quickly, then slipped it back into his wallet.

"No," he said. "You don't want to see her picture."

"I don't mind, if you'd like to show it to me." She felt he was acting strangely—almost as if he were afraid. "Why don't you describe her to me?"

"She was lovely."

"I can imagine."

"She had a pretty oval face, like yours. But her hair was naturally blond."

"You don't like my hair? I've been thinking of changing it."

"It's not your natural hair."

Tiny found herself smiling. He had a sort of creepy charm.

"Would you have dinner with me some night?"

"Oh, I can't do that—not ever."

"How about meeting me here? Tomorrow's a good time."

"No, I can't. I really have to go." She put a bill down upon the bar, waited for her change from Nick, then found herself smiling at Harry again. "Thanks for the wisdom; it was therapeutic."

"One more bit. You can never leave someone about whom your feelings are ambivalent."

"Explain it to me."

"No, you'll have to come to understand those words yourself."

"I like it and I don't like it. I really have to go. Thank you again."

She walked along Madison toward Fifty-seventh Street and the building she lived in. A strange man. All the while he had talked with her she had not felt the presence. But now it was back again—in full force.

She must look around and prove to herself he wasn't there.

This time there *was* someone there. Harry walking toward her, Harry tipping his hat.

Tiny put her fist in her mouth to keep from whimpering, then turned and fled into the arms of her welcoming doorman.

2

Harry Barratt's heart was pounding. Take it easy, old man! You've thought you've been sure before, only to be mistaken over and over again. But he knew, knew down deep inside him that this time, at last, he had found his long-lost Tiny.

Be careful, don't be impetuous, don't frighten her off. She can't know anything about your existence. Follow your plan in every detail, but don't improvise—it could be disastrous. And above all, be circumspect, especially in the pivotal stage, where an uninformed observer might take your actions to be criminal.

Criminal! The very thought was loathsome. He had come to know from bitter experience that evil existed as a constant threat to good in this world, but his love for Tiny, his dedication to her salvation, placed him above and beyond such considerations. By his act, indeed, he would snatch her from the evildoers as they had taken her from him—he would restore her to his world of spiritual health and loving kindness, to wholesome values and self-respect.

Harry's step quickened as he neared the florist shop toward which he had been striding purposively ever since

Tiny had glimpsed him again outside the entrance to the apartment building. He went inside and ordered from the shopkeeper a dozen white roses, the essence of purity. He wrote "From your Harry" on a card and told the man he would take them with him.

As soon as he left the florist shop, he strode back the several blocks to the apartment building he had seen Tiny enter. A fearsome thought occurred to him. She might not reside there, might only be visiting a friend. But the doorman had obviously known her, called her "Miss Barratt." That was all that mattered.

The man was standing inside the foyer. He opened the door for Harry and accepted the long white box tied with a bow of white satin ribbon—for which Harry had paid extra.

"Will you please see to it that Miss Barratt receives those at once!" Harry said in his most authoritarian manner. And he slipped the doorman a five-dollar bill.

"I will take them up to the penthouse personally, sir."

Harry smiled as he walked to Madison Avenue, where he had parked his car. He hoped the meter hadn't run out. Oh, well, he had a Pennsylvania license. If he got a ticket, he could throw it away.

Good luck! There were five minutes of unexpired time on the meter. He unlocked the car and drove back to East Fifty-seventh Street and to a garage he had noticed there, and told the attendant that he would not be needing his car until the next day. Before he gave the garageman his key, he unlocked the trunk and tugged out a heavy pigskin two-suiter, which was well-scuffed but still handsome.

When he reached the street, he looked around at the nearby hotels on the south side of the avenue, counting their stories. The Grovenor was a satisfactory thirty stories high; Tiny's building had only twenty floors. He crossed the street against the light, cabs honking at him, and hurried along to the hotel.

"I want a room, preferably a suite, high up," he said to the desk clerk.

"Yes, sir; 2504 is available."

"Does that have a northern exposure?"

"All our suites have a northern exposure, sir."

"Fine. I'll take it."

"How long is your stay, sir?" the room clerk asked as Harry signed the register.

"A day or so."

"That will be fifty-eight dollars a day including taxes, sir. Payable in advance."

Harry placed a hundred-dollar bill on the counter and took his change, then followed the bellman to the elevator.

The suite consisted of a large, high-ceilinged living room, rather ornately furnished in the style of a much earlier time, a bedroom and a bath. There were two windows facing on Fifty-seventh Street. While the bellman was turning on lights and struggling to lift Harry's heavy bag onto the rack, Harry went to the window and peered across the street. Five stories down, the penthouse and its terrace were in plain view.

"Is everything all right, sir?"

Harry nodded his head and gave the man a dollar. Alone in the suite, he did not unpack but paced for about five minutes, frequently consulting his wrist watch. Then he went to the desk and opened the Manhattan classified telephone directory, thumbing its pages for a few minutes until he found what he wanted. He grabbed up the key the bellman had dropped on the desk, left the suite, slamming the door, and lunged down the corridor to the elevator. When he reached the street, he hailed a cab and told the driver to take him to Abercrombie & Fitch. At the huge sporting goods store, he left the cab as hurriedly as he had taken it, rushed inside and asked where he might buy binoculars.

The salesman in the department was busy with another customer and Harry Barratt began to drum on the counter with his fingernails. Both customer and clerk glanced at him in annoyance, but Harry didn't notice. Finally, the transaction completed, the salesman approached him.

"I want some binoculars. High magnification."

"Domestic or foreign, sir?"

"I don't care, just as long as there is no ambivalence."

"We don't stock ambivalent binoculars, sir."

The clerk was looking at him strangely, but Harry didn't care. He wasn't about to explain to a salesman how the ambivalence between good and evil created all the destructive forces in the world. He seized the binoculars the clerk handed him, and going to the window facing Madison Avenue, focused the glasses on one of the windows across the way. He was looking over the shoulder of the typist and could just make out some of the words she was typing. Ambivalence!

"Those are our very finest binoculars. May I suggest a telescope."

"Aah!"

Harry took the telescope and repeated his previous act; this time he could clearly read every word the secretary was typing.

"I'll take it."

"Cash or charge?"

"Cash."

After some figuring, the clerk said, "That'll be $279.97, sir, with tax."

Harry gave the man three hundred-dollar bills, and drummed on the counter again until the fellow brought his package. Then he paced impatiently until the elevator came and once down, pushed his way out of the store, hailing the first taxi that came along even though it was going in the wrong direction.

"I can't make no right until Sixth, buddy, then I'll have to take you all the way back past Madison on Fifty-seventh. Now, if you took a cab across the street—"

"It doesn't matter. Get going!" Harry shouted at the cabby.

As the driver had predicted, the route was needlessly roundabout and since traffic was heavy on both Sixth Avenue and Fifty-seventh Street, it took twenty minutes to reach the hotel. The fare was five dollars. Harry threw a five-dollar bill through the partition, grabbed his package and jumped out of the cab.

As soon as he reached the suite, Harry unwrapped the telescope and focused it on the penthouse across the street. He scanned each window, but the blinds were drawn and he couldn't see inside even though he felt he could reach out and touch the window, could rap on it.

He swiveled the 'scope on its stand and began to pan the terrace. He gasped. Lying on a beach chair was a beautiful woman, almost totally nude. Her bronzed body was covered only at breasts and groin by a scant bikini the size of three small handkerchiefs. Her eyes were closed but he recognized with a shock the platinum-blond hair, the oval face, the long, lissome body of his Tiny.

She had really fallen into evil hands. Little wonder she had wept.

Harry Barratt began to cry too, clenching his hands into fists and beating them upon his chest.

It was a quarter of an hour before his rage subsided. Then he went to the telephone and gave the operator a number. "May I speak to Julio? This is Harry Barratt.

. . . Julio? Did you get the memorandum of deposit?

He heard a grunt of assent.

"Always glad to do you and the organization a favor. I discounted ten percent into my own account as per our agreement. . . . Right. Now *I* want a favor. I want to lease an apartment in 259 East 57th Street. . . . Right. As close to the top floor as possible. I want the contractors to do the standard job. Soundproof. Windows you can see out of but you can't see into. . . . Oh, the nineteenth floor—already set up? How soon can you move the girls out? . . . The end of the weekend will be wonderful. O.K., then move out all their furniture, clothes, cancel the phone. I'll just take over the lease. . . . A Mr. Randall? Right. And have the contractors furnish it all in white. Sofas. Beds. Paint the walls white. The kitchen cabinets. The whole bit. Really *white.* I want to move in by the end of next week."

3

As the elevator sped upward, Tiny felt the force of the evil presence dwindle until by the time the door opened on the twentieth floor and she climbed the short flight of stairs to the penthouse, it had vanished and she began to breathe easily. An evil presence or the presence of evil? Whichever it was, it couldn't derive entirely from the presence of the man who called himself Harry, because she had first sensed it in the doctor's office, had sensed it there many times before. Or could it? Had the other occurrences of that presence been premonitions, warnings of the meeting with the man himself that was about to occur?

He had seemed a genial, pleasant older man who had been genuinely concerned about her emotional state— hardly the way one would expect evil to present itself. Yet soon after she had left Once Over Lightly she had felt the presence again, felt its force slowly increasing. When, in front of her building, she had turned to confront whatever it was, there had been Harry, smiling and tipping his hat! It was puzzling.

She turned on the lights in the living room—Joel insisted on keeping the blinds drawn—and saw all the familiar objects of their collection. The rack, the whips, the thumbscrew, the boot, the Iron Maiden. She walked over to the rack and ran her hand lovingly along its surface. It was an excellent replica of an example from the early seventeenth century in France that Joel had discovered in the *oubliette* of a château in Burgundy. Hundreds of times she had lain on it, green and blue spots playing on her, as they closed the show with their number The Rack and the Maiden. As the tension increased and it was obvious that her muscles and tendons were being stretched, a curtain fell, only to rise again moments later, and she would be standing beside the rack, bowing to the audience, while Joel would be on the rack, writhing in mock agony.

It was an illusion that none of their competitors had been able to imitate because they lacked the contortionist skills Joel and Uncle Eddie had taught her when she was a little girl. And it was one of the reasons the act was in such demand for club dates and conventions, at resorts and in nightclubs: it combined the mystery of illusion with the spine-tingling titivation and decadent eroticism of Grand Guignol.

She felt safe again. The presence was never felt in the penthouse. What would I do if it invaded my home? I mustn't even think of it. This may not have anything to do with Harry, or any other man; it may be just a projection of my own thoughts.

She went into her bedroom, and took off her clothes and

stood in front of the pier glass admiring her long, full-breasted body, even cupping her hand for a moment over the mound of blond pubic hair. "Daddy, Daddy, you're right," she said in a whisper to her mirror. "I *am* beautiful!"

Men must like her. She could feel their eyes upon her during the act. She could feel Harry's eyes upon her. She enjoyed the sensation. Why must she be the way she was?

There came into her mind a glimmering of something Harry had said. Something about ambivalence. Now she couldn't remember it all. "I'll take a nice warm bath; that's what I need," she confided to the mirror.

In the tub with the warm but not hot water caressing her, she felt whole again. There was no presence, only herself and the loving warm water, but she did not allow herself to linger too long in the bath. She needed the sun.

Rubbing herself dry on a huge bath towel, Tiny walked naked into her bedroom and found in the drawer of her chest her scantiest, naughtiest bikini. She had just finished fitting it over her ample breasts and thighs when she heard the buzzer ring.

She picked up the phone of the intercom. "Yes?"

"I have a package for madame. May I bring it up?" It was the darling old doorman.

"Of course, Ernst."

She went into the living room to wait for his delivery, first putting on her terry-cloth robe. Ernst knew she was show-biz, but even at his age he might get ideas.

He was at the penthouse door in a minute. He offered her a long white carton. "From a gentleman."

"What gentleman?"

"He didn't leave his name, madame."

"Thank you, Ernst."

After the door closed, Tiny opened the florist's box. A dozen beautiful pure-white roses! Lovely! Joel always gave her blood-red American Beauties. So they couldn't be from Joel, although sending flowers was just like him, with her doing the Iron Maiden on TV tonight. She searched for a card. "From your Harry."

She felt the presence again, stealthy and far away—but for the first time it had invaded her home.

She screamed.

4

"You can never leave someone about whom your feelings are ambivalent." That was what Harry had said. And now the flowers. How did the remark, the gift, the transitory feeling of the presence—it had disappeared entirely now— how did they all fit together?

Tiny couldn't even guess at the answer, but she knew there was some connection, some plausible, or possibly implausible, explanation. She gathered the roses from the box and put them with fresh water into a crystal vase. Then she went out onto the terrace to sun herself until Joel arrived.

It was a good idea. As soon as she stretched out upon the beach chair with the warmth of the sun on her body, she felt once again back in touch with her real self. What had happened in the doctor's office, her meeting with Harry, her concern about the presence, the unexpected gift of flowers —none of these things seemed really important any longer. All that mattered was that she was here, on her own terrace, warm in the sun, safe, safe, safe.

She remembered how it had been when as a little girl— she was three or three and a half, certainly less than four —she had come home from the hospital after having had polio. She had still been in pain, and Joel had taken her to the beach every day and made her lie in the sun, even after its rays baked into her body and made it hurt in a different way—made her wait until the tide rose and the cool waves lapped at her burning flesh. "You must be patient," he had kept saying. 'You must not give up. You must endure."

Later there had been the daily trips to see Uncle Eddie, who had made her do exercises that hurt. He was a tall man with a swarthy complexion and bushy hair—with lots of even bushier hair on his chest, which was always exposed —who every afternoon showed her the tricks he did on the trapeze, but only when she had completed her exercises. He and his wife, Molly, swung back and forth from the trapezes after Molly returned from her job at the aircraft plant. Uncle Eddie and Molly would collapse, panting and sweating, afterward, and Uncle Eddie would say to her: "You do the exercises as you did today and when you grow up and Molly is too old, you'll be my partner in the act." Then he would put his arm around his wife, hug her, and say, "I only married her because all the other acts were after her, and if I married her the other guys wouldn't have a chance." Even then Tiny had known he was kidding.

But after all, it was Uncle Eddie who had given her the name she was known by in show biz, Tiny. Her real name was Sheila, but hardly anybody called her that. *"Tiny"* was splendidly inappropriate to her—five-ten and with a good figure. She remembered how it had come about.

It was the first time Joel had taken her to the beach house at Santa Monica where Uncle Eddie and Aunt Molly lived. Joel had carried her from the car. Uncle Eddie had come running to meet them, his arms out. He had grasped her, cuddled her to his hairy breast. She could still feel the warmth of his flesh, the smell of his sun-baked sweat as he held her tight against him. She could still hear the rumble of his voice.

"My God, Joel, you want me to teach this child to be a contortionist? She's so tiny."

"The doctor says it's either that or Sister Kenny."

It was with Uncle Eddie, and then later with Joel, that she had learned to persist, to stay with whatever she attempted, to linger, to circle, slowly to come down and seize, hawk-like, that which she wanted to be her own.

There had never been a presence then. Only a feeling of contest against her physical limitations, long since successful, yet continuing—and a sense of being loved, watched over, guarded.

And a desire to escape.

"Why can't you just leave?" the psychiatrist had asked.

"The act?"

"If that's what you need to leave."

"I couldn't."

"Why? It's not the money?"

"No, it's because then . . . then I'd be alone."

What kind of answer was that? At the very moment she had been answering Dr. Feldman's questions, what had been most on her mind was the presence she felt behind her. And the true reason she had told him she could not leave Joel . . . she had lied about pretending it was a true reason. Sometimes she thought she must be going mad. Reasons . . . what were reasons? There was the presence. There was the sense of lying here being one with the sun. There were Joel and, off somewhere, Uncle Eddie and Aunt Molly.

She knew there should be more. She was twenty-five, a beautiful woman, an accomplished artist, a magician. Yet she felt safe and content only when she was alone with the sun. It was why she had persuaded Joel to make their professional dates in Florida and California in the winter. Well, it was good business too.

She changed her position, opened her eyes, lifted her sunglasses. Looking upward, she saw a brief glint from one of the upper windows of the Hotel Grovenor across the street.

Another dirty old man with binoculars. Well, let him have a good look!

5

Harry had tried to stay away from the window. He had set up his plan; it would work through. Now he would have to be patient. He knew enough about an operation to realize that what led to failure was acting on impulse, trying to bring about the desired result before it was possible according to the plan. Ambivalence—it invariably led to mistakes, to wrongdoing, to evil!

He knew all this, yet he took out the telescope, set it up on its stand, parted the blinds, focused it upon the terrace. The young woman was still there, all but unclothed, his Tiny! She seemed so close to him that he wanted to pick her up in his arms and fondle her. He remembered the last time he had seen her, before he had gone off to work that morning. She had been so small, but so like Muriel. He had plucked her from her crib to kiss her and had felt her cheek burning against his own. "Muriel, she has a fever!" he had cried.

His wife had said drowsily from bed, "Only a cold. Harry, you better go. You'll be late."

The last time he had seen her—until now. He examined her through the 'scope, tracing her long, ample form from her toes up her thighs to her breasts, her throat, her face. He saw her flip down her sunglasses and look upward, directly at him. His heart stopped. But she couldn't have seen him! Then she shrugged, and turned her head aside.

His own Tiny! It wouldn't be long now. A week at most.

Harry was about to stop watching—the use of the telescope made him feel guilty, though he knew it was justified —then he saw a man come out on the terrace. A tall man with long, wavy gray hair, wearing a full-dress evening suit and looking diabolical. He approached Tiny. (He had called her Tiny from the first instant that he had seen her in the maternity ward of the hospital: she had been so small, so helpless.) The man, the Devil, approached his Tiny. He began to talk to her. Tiny jumped up, her breasts for a moment bobbing out of her brief bathing attire.

They were arguing.

God knew what the Devil wanted her to do!

Joel came out on the terrace in full costume. That meant he was ready for them to start rehearsing. Tiny glanced at her watch and saw that they wouldn't be taping for another couple of hours. She yawned. She would like a nap. A little nap would be nice.

"I thought you'd be ready."

"But it's only three-thirty."

"You know we're doing the Iron Maiden tonight. I already have it loaded in the van. I wouldn't want anything to go wrong."

"Nothing is going wrong, Daddy. You worry too much." He was as handsome as ever and seemed to grow younger with the years. She liked his wavy gray hair, his trim mustache, the diabolical twinkle in his blue-gray eyes. Joel was always on stage.

"I saw Manny today. He's booked us into Baltimore for two shows next Friday. The first starts at seven, then one at eleven. Rehearsal is at five. We'll have to leave at noon."

"Daddy, you know I can't! My doctor's appointment is at eleven!"

"You can skip him one week. I'm not even sure he's doing you any good."

She knew his prejudice against psychiatrists. But he had no right to take a date that conflicted with the one important appointment of her week. She flared up. "The act is always making me change my life. I can't go out with a man at a decent hour because we have a rehearsal, or you've taken a date at the last moment. I can't see friends. No wonder I'm so unpopular."

"Is that what your shrink says—that the act is interfering with your love life?"

"No, he didn't say that."

"What did he say?"

"He is never directive—he never tells me what to do."

"What did he say that has you so upset?"

"It's nothing he said that has me upset. It's you and your interference. Daddy, I'm going to put my foot down. I'm not going to Baltimore with you next Friday. We don't need one date so much and you know it." She was calm now, determined, her anger spent.

"What did the shrink say?"

"He didn't tell me anything. You don't understand. He asks questions and I have to find the answers, hard answers."

"What questions did he ask?"

"He asked me why I couldn't just leave."

"Leave what? The act? Me?"

"He didn't say. I asked him if he meant the act. He said, 'If that's what you need to leave.'"

"Sounds like rubbish to me. He should come out and say what he means in no uncertain terms. You can leave if you

want. I can train another assistant. You're not indispensable."

She stood up and threw her arms around him, hugged
him. "Oh, Daddy, I'm not going to leave the act and you
know it! Now I'm going in and put on my costume and we
can go to rehearsal."

"You can leave if you want. I mean it."

"Daddy, I'm not going to leave the act. It's my identity."

6

Convinced by the colloquy he had glimpsed, if not over-
heard, that his Tiny was really in the hands of Beelzebub,
Harry collapsed on his bed. There was nothing he could do
for a week. She would have to remain in perfidy! Later he
would go back through his files and attempt to identify the
human form Satan had taken—he might find the clue to the
entire mystery!—but now he knew his only recourse was
sleep, then a drink or two, a sound dinner . . . and the files.

Harry slept like the dead, awakening at dusk on a long
summer's evening. It was eight-thirty! He jumped up,
stripped off his clothes, showered, dug into his suitcase for
another suit, shirt, tie, socks. Refreshed, he thought of
calling room service, but decided he needed better than
that. He went down to the street and took a cab to the
Russian Tea Room, where he dined sumptuously.

It was clear that if he was to save his Tiny, he must hold
to his plan. Don't be impetuous, don't improvise, don't
frighten her off. Above all, don't give the Devil a clue. He
kept nodding his head to his own self-remonstrances, and
ordering cup after cup of tea.

He paid his check and took a stroll to Central Park in the
languorous night air. He knew it was dangerous to be in the

park this late, so he stayed near the exits and walked back to the hotel before he was ready. In the room again, he emptied the bottom of his valise of the cram of newspaper and magazine clippings, the photos and photostats of dossiers, all his files on Tiny. He went through the entire mass of material three times: he found no halftone or photo that resembled the face of His Satanic Majesty's representation on this earth that he had scrutinized through the telescope. The mystery remained.

He lay back on the chair, a cigarette alight—his first of the day—and pondered.

There ought to be some action he could take that would make his intervention between Tiny and her victimizer more effective, more prompt. He could call Julio again, but no, he didn't want Julio and his people to know more of his business.

All he could do was to keep up his surveillance through the telescope day by day. If at any time he saw that he must take immediate action, he would do what had to be done then. It was the only prudent course.

Sighing, he stood up and walked to the television set, turning it on. Another instrument of the Devil! He sat in the easy chair and watched it flickering, not bothering to flip the dials—he would watch whatever came on.

He heard a lugubrious voice, saw a shock of wavy gray hair framing glittering eyes, a pasty complexion, a blood-red mouth. The Devil! Even on television! Dumbstruck, he listened. "And now we come to the final scene of 'The Perils of Tiny'—'The Iron Maiden.' Although I assure my viewers that the Iron Maiden is authentic, an exactly accurate replica of an ancient torture device I discovered in a Spanish castle—no doubt a relic of the Inquisition"—he gave a grisly laugh—"I want to reassure you that Tiny will come to no harm. Indeed, she will be back next week for

21

another gruesome episode. And now, Tiny in the clutches of the Iron Maiden. She has been a very naughty girl, you see, and her liege lord will put up with her errant behavior no longer." Another grisly laugh. 'She is to be put to death in the bosom of the Iron Maiden. . . .''

The camera panned away from the Devil's face to a close-up of *his* Tiny, her face as pale as the ghost he feared she might become despite Satan's reassurances, her eyes large, her mouth trembling. She was manacled. Brawny hands seized her. She was dragged toward the torture machine of iron, a gross representation of a woman on the outside, but now agape to reveal the spikes with deadly points that lined the inside of the pseudo sculpture's breasts, womb, thighs.

Tiny screamed, "No, no, I won't be bad again! No, no, not that!"

Sweat beaded Harry's face, his palms were clammy. He was remembering another time, another place, hearing Tiny cry out, "No, no, I won't be bad again! No, no, not that!"

And he watched the brawny arms force Tiny into the killing embrace, saw the doors close . . . and felt faint.

Then he saw Tiny, an instant later, spring from the machine, laughingly wiping the bloodstains from her body.

2

A WEEK LATER

Tiny arrived at her doctor's office the following Friday at the appointed hour. She had only to wait a few minutes. When Dr. Feldman opened his door, she gathered up her purse, replaced the copy of *Psychology Today* she had been thumbing through, and went right in. She shook his hand as he stood—she liked the fact that he had a firm, dry hand —and seated herself on the couch. She never lay upon it. She had asked at the beginning whether she must and he had told her to do whatever was comfortable.

"You know, Tiny, of all my patients you are the only one who invariably shakes my hand when you meet me and when you leave."

"Invariably? You mean there are some who do it sometimes?"

"Exactly. I have my hands wrung at times."

"That must be uncomfortable. But to shake hands is only manners, surely?"

"Manners, yes. But also acceptance."

"Oh, I accept you. Do I accept you! I am here in defiance of my father."

"He didn't want you to come?"

"Well, as you know, he hasn't really bought the whole idea from the beginning. And yes, he didn't want me to come today. But it wasn't because he objects to my visiting you. It's only that he had taken a date in Baltimore for tonight and he wanted me to break our appointment. I put my foot down. I told him I was going to keep my appointment and he would just have to get somebody else to be his assistant.

"Of course, she won't be able to do the rack or the Iron Maiden, and probably not the levitation—though he has been rehearsing her all week for that—but he has a lot of other props and gimmicks. I'm not indispensable. And he has to realize, sooner or later, that I have my life to live. Everything isn't the act."

"How does it feel?"

"How does what feel?"

"To put your foot down?"

"Wonderful. I've loved every minute of it. I met a man."

"Before you put your foot down?"

"Yes."

"What kind of a man?"

"Middle-aged."

"Did you feel differently this time?"

"I don't know what you mean."

"You came to me, Tiny, because despite all your show-business sophistication, you couldn't relate to a man. In the presence of an eligible man you became frightened. You had even gone to the ladies' room in a fashionable restaurant and tipped the washroom attendant to let you out the back way."

"Yes."

"And we have gone into your love for your father, your knowledge that he isn't really your natural father, but the man who married your mother and took care of you; how

24

in your teens you had to take over as his assistant in the act after your mother's untimely death; how this made you feel guilty about leaving him—even for an evening with another man."

. "Yes. What are you asking me?"

"I'm asking you if you felt this way with the man you say you met 'before you put your foot down'?"

"I don't know. I don't know how to answer you."

"Would you like to tell me something about this man?"

"He's middle-aged."

"Yes. What is his name?"

"Harry."

"Where did you meet him?"

"In a bar—right after I saw you last Friday."

"You went to a bar after seeing me?"

"Yes. Is that so dreadful? I usually go to that bar. I have a drink and I weep. The bartender is very nice. He said to me last Friday, 'It isn't the end of the world.' "

"Do you think the bartender was right?"

"That it isn't the end of the world?"

"Yes."

"I'd never thought of it."

"Think of it."

"You mean it could be the end of the world—my world?"

"You came in here saying you had put your foot down. And I asked you how it felt."

"I said wonderful. You mean I've taken the first step toward leaving the act—for good. Yes, I suppose I have. He was very kind. He offered me a cocktail napkin to dry my eyes."

"The middle-aged man?"

"No, silly, the bartender. Oh, I'm sorry, doctor; I didn't mean to say you're silly."

"Sometimes I am."

"No; I didn't realize Harry was sitting next to me until after that. He must have seen that I was crying, too. I was out of cigarettes and I asked him for one."

"Then what happened?"

"He asked me something about . . . something about why I was troubled and would it help if I talked about it to him. I said no and I turned away from him. And then I realized that I did need, really need, to talk to a man."

"Ah!"

"What?"

"Nothing."

"You said something you didn't want me to hear?"

"I sighed, my dear. I have heartburn sometimes. What did you say to this middle-aged man when you realized that you needed to talk to a man?"

"I said I'd be glad to listen to his troubles."

"And did he tell you of them?"

"Yes."

"What were they?"

"Something about his wife—he called her a runaway bride. He said it was hard at first, it was like death; that he cried, 'My God, why did this have to happen to me?' Then there was a period of mourning—then at last, acceptance. Then he asked me out to dinner."

"Did you enjoy dinner with him?"

"Of course not. I didn't accept his invitation. I said 'I can't' to him."

"But why not?"

"You know I can't have dinner with a man. It's why I came to see you."

"Do you want to see him again?"

"I don't know. Oh, I did see him again. Not long after I left the bar, but before that . . ."

"Yes?"

"He said the strangest thing to me. I asked him to explain it, but he said I'd have to try to understand the words myself."

"What did he say?"

"He said, 'You can never leave someone about whom your feelings are ambivalent.' Doctor, what does that mean?"

"It means that if you have mixed feelings about another person you cannot make up your mind about that person."

"Do you think that's true?"

"In some cases, yes."

"In my case?"

"Possibly. It depends on the person. You left this man—what was his name?"

"Harry. Oh, yes, I left him a few minutes later. I thanked him for cheering me, but I left. I had to—we had a rehearsal. And I needed some rest. But he followed me."

"He followed you?"

"To the door of my apartment building. I turned around and saw him."

"What did he do?"

"He smiled and tipped his hat."

"What did you do?"

"I went into the building as fast as I could. . . . Doctor?"

"Yes?"

"There's something more I should tell you."

"Yes?"

"A half hour or so later the doorman brought up a dozen white roses, beautiful roses, with a card—'From your Harry.' "

"This gentleman's feelings are not ambivalent about you," the doctor said. And then, "Tiny, your time is up."

"Already?"

"I can give you a few more minutes."

27

I haven't told him about the presence. Oh, how can I even begin in so short a time?

"There is something that's bothering you?"

"Doctor, for the first time, the first time at home, I mean —I've felt it here, I've felt it on the street, almost anywhere, but never at home—I felt the *presence.*"

"The 'presence'?"

"I haven't told you about it, have I?"

"No, I don't think you have."

"It's a feeling of evil behind me—always behind me. I don't know what it is. Oh, I know it sounds silly, but it isn't —it's dreadful!"

"You say you've felt it here?"

"Just last Friday, only then—as always before—when I looked around there was nothing there: only you."

"Only I was there—as always before?"

"Usually nothing—nobody. That once, just that once— you. It's why I wept in the bar. I could feel the presence. Then . . . then Harry began to talk to me, and it disappeared. Only when I left him, left the bar, I began to feel it again. And when I turned around, he was there. And later, upstairs, when I was home, and the doorman brought up the white roses, the beautiful white roses, I felt it again."

"You think this presence has to do with Harry, with me, with your father?"

"Do you think it could?"

"It might. Tiny, why don't you go have a drink with your friend at the bar?"

"Harry?"

"Yes."

"Do you think he'll be there?"

"Yes, he might."

"But then I'll feel the presence again?"

"Have you felt it here?"

"No, not today."

"Then that eliminates one of us, doesn't it? Tiny, your time is up."

2

Harry hadn't counted on a female interior decorator. Even now he didn't know if it had been a trick of Julio's or if she was only the person who was in right with the organization. He had called Julio Thursday morning, as he had each day of the week, and been told by his secretary that the apartment would be ready after three that afternoon. "Just tell the doorman you have an appointment with Mr. Randall."

Mr. Randall was a small, balding, officious man, who had been most obsequious. "19M? Yes, indeed. I believe it is quite ready. I'm sure you will be enthusiastic, Mr. Barratt. This envelope contains two sets of keys. I'd like to show you up personally."

They had taken the elevator to the nineteenth floor. The door of 19M had been standing open and Harry had remarked on it. "But those were the instructions; very explicit," Mr. Randall said. "Only you can open that door or close it, or whoever you give the key to—look and see."

Harry had opened the envelope, which he had stuffed in his pocket. The "keys" were pieces of plastic bearing symbols printed in magnetic ink. Mr. Randall showed him how to fit the plastic card into a thin slot on the door and how it activated the dead bolt. "Pickproof," he said proudly.

"There's no such thing as a pickproof lock," Harry said, though he was impressed by Julio's ingenuity.

Harry shook Mr. Randall's hand and closed the door on him. The apartment's foyer was shining white and mirrored on either wall, with console tables upon which were white

29

porcelain vases filled with long-stemmed lilies. "Very nice." The living room was long, high-ceilinged, its broad windows draped with white velvet. The wall-to-wall carpeting was white shag; the coffee table was mirrored, but the conversational grouping of sofas about the white onyx fireplace showed the prevailing absence of all color, as did the white-on-white painting in a platinum frame above it.

Harry, whistling, had walked into the dining room: a Parsons table and executive-type swivel chairs, all pure white. He pushed through the door into the kitchen; the wall oven, refrigerator and freezer, counter, sink—everything was immaculately white. So was the bathroom, with its sunken tub and stall shower. He'd returned to the inner hall and gone into the bedrooms. There were three small ones, any of which would be suitable for him—really more bedrooms than necessary, but then one can't have everything—all in white, of course. The master bedroom, Tiny's room, was truly beautiful. The walls were upholstered with tufted white satin; on the vanity was an array of crystal and white marble; there were mirrors on each wall, soft lights, deep, furlike carpeting; and upon the heart-shaped bed, having thrown back the ermine comforter, lay the most beautiful black woman he had ever seen, totally naked, legs spread, welcoming him.

Harry had thrown himself upon her avidly. They had made love all afternoon, all night. He had had to beg her to leave an hour ago.

She had been beautiful, though. Lucille. He had her phone number. She wanted to see him tonight, but that, of course, was impossible. Though he would see her again. There was no way she could understand the mission that intervened, even between himself and her, the mission which was his first responsibility. A woman could never understand the ideal, the missed opportunity which must be restored if a man was to regain himself. A woman could never understand ambivalence.

Why were these ideas beyond the mental capacity of womankind? Harry had stripped the stained sheets from the bed and was now neatly putting fresh satin sheets upon it. Women prided themselves on facing the facts of life, on being in touch with reality, they sneered at men for being what they called "romantic"—yet they could never understand how infected they were by their own ambivalence.

Even his own Tiny. At first she would not want to accept the fact that her own father, her real father, had finally found her, that he was going to seize her from the forces of evil in which she had been nurtured, return her to the breast of humankind. You would think she would sense her good fortune, would have known it at their first meeting, when he had spoken to her so eloquently, though cautiously, guardedly, only hinting—from bitter experience—of the truth and where it led. Even so, though he perceived that she had sensed a part, if not all, of what he was trying to impress upon her, she had left him. And when he had followed her, and she had confronted him, she had appeared about to scream—as if he threatened her, her own long-lost father!

Yet he had seen her on TV that same night, caught up in the devices of the Devil. He had seen her emerge from the Iron Maiden, wearing only that bikini, bleeding from the lacerations the implement of torture had inflicted upon her—smiling and cavorting and pretending she was not in pain. He had called the TV station at once to protest, had spoken to one of its employees. The man had said, "I know it's very realistic, sir, but it's only an illusion. Most of our viewers like it—in fact, they have the best Nielsen for this time of night all week. However, if you wish to protest, I suggest you write a postcard to our station at—"

Harry had hung up on him. He had known then that he must remember his plan, be patient, and not let anyone "out there" have any information about his rescue and rehabilitation program for Tiny. He must not be impetuous. He must take every step along the way as he had plotted it. It was her only salvation.

He had finished tidying up and it was almost noon. He had to catch a cab and go to Once Over Lightly.

Tiny might be there.

3

Nick was alone behind the bar when Tiny came in. "The usual?"

"Scotch with a twist. Water on the side. Yes."

"You're feeling better?"

"I'm feeling aces. I put my foot down."

"Sometimes that's a good idea."

"And sometimes it's not?"

"*Comme ci, comme ça.*"

"Well, it's definitely *comme ci* as far as I'm concerned."

"At least you know you have a foot," Nick said.

"Right. It's nice to have a foot. A foot to put down."

Nick polished a glass.

"It makes you know where you are. That you are," Tiny said.

A man came into the bar. The man Tiny had been expecting. Harry. He had lipstick on his face. Not only smeared on his mouth, but on his cheek, forehead and throat. Dark, crimson, glossy lipstick. He sat beside Tiny.

"You aren't weeping today?"

"I'm laughing."

"It's the reverse of tears."

"What?"

"Laughter."

Nick placed his hands on the bar. "Why don't you go into the bathroom and look at yourself before you talk to this lady?"

Harry stared at him, rubbed his face with his hand, then went to the men's room.

"You think he's all right?" Tiny asked Nick.

"I think he's all right. He's just been on a drunk."

"Why do men act like that?"

"Like what?"

"Go out and get drunk? Get lipstick on themselves?"

"Lady, if I could tell you that, I wouldn't be a bartender."

"But you do know."

"I suppose, from your point of view, I do."

"What do you mean—from my point of view?"

"Just what I said."

"You mean the way I look at things is different from the way you, as a male, as a bartender, look at things?"

"Yes."

"I wish I could see me from your point of view."

"You're an attractive, intelligent, cultured young woman," Nick said. "You're too hard on yourself, though. You have a problem, and because you have this problem, you're too hard on yourself. But it's not a unique problem —in fact, it's a problem most young women have sooner or later in their lives."

"And you know what this problem is?"

"Sure."

"Then tell me."

"You don't have a man."

"You think it's as simple as that?"

"Nothing is ever simple."

Tiny shoved her empty glass toward him. He put some

rocks in it and some Scotch. "Good luck!"

"Well, in a way you're right."

"You don't have a man?"

"No. I don't. But it's not as simple as that."

Harry came rushing out of the men's room. He sat in the barber chair beside hers and seized both her hands in his clenched, perspiring palms. "Forgive me, dearest—oh, please forgive me," he implored her.

Tiny withdrew her hands. She suppressed a grimace of distaste.

"Please, forgive me," he said again.

"For what?"

"Let's not think of it, or mention it again," Harry said.

"Think of what?" Tiny asked, but he had jumped up, run to the door, disappeared.

"What's the matter with him?"

Nick shook his head. "Lady, sometimes I think we have an invisible magnet in here that works only on the nuts, the screwballs, who walk by on the street. It draws them right in."

"You think he's a nut? But he was so nice to me last week."

"Nuts can be nice. He can have a screw loose and still be nice."

"I suppose you think I'm a nut too, weeping all the time."

"You haven't wept today."

"No, but I might start."

"Are you threatening me?"

Tiny laughed. "Hardly."

"All I know about you is that last week you thought it was the end of the world, whatever had happened or hadn't happened."

"Hadn't happened."

"Now look at you. Tell me—what happened?"

"I told you. I put my foot down."

"That's all?"

"That's all. But I'd never done it before, you see. That's what made it so difficult. But I did it, at last. I was supposed to be in Baltimore today, with the act. But I had an appointment, a very important appointment. I said no. I never had before, but I said no. He's going to have to do the act this time with somebody else. He's been rehearsing her all week."

Nick smiled and, momentarily, covered his eyes with his hand. "I knew you looked familiar. All this time I've been telling myself, 'She looks familiar!' Now I think I know. You're the Maiden—on TV."

"Yes, I am," Tiny said. "But you're the first one to recognize me in the longest time. The make-up makes me look different, I guess, and the costumes, the props."

"Would you have dinner with me tonight?" Nick asked. "I'm off here at six o'clock. I could pick you up, or we could meet, or you could come to my place."

Tiny felt the presence again. She was looking directly at Nick, but she felt the presence behind her. "Are you the presence?"

"Well, I'm present. Have dinner with me tonight."

"I have this creepy feeling, at times, that there's a presence behind me, watching me." Tiny felt she was about to lose her balance. This was it. This was the test. If she said no, she would remain right where she had always been. If she said yes . . .

"I'll take care of your 'presence,'" Nick said.

"Yes. Your place," she whispered.

"Tell me more about this 'presence.'"

Tiny had another Scotch with Nick and probably talked too much about her peculiar fear of the presence. Then she left for an appointment with her hairdresser. She had gone into the bar expecting possibly to see Harry, half-decided, because of what Dr. Feldman had said about a lack of ambivalence on Harry's part, that if he asked her out again she would accept. Harry had rushed in, looking comic—some other woman had obviously been kissing him—then had rushed out foolishly. And now she was going to have dinner with the bartender at his place. Joel should see her now! She had a date with a man!

As she left the hairdresser's, Tiny glanced at her watch. Five o'clock; she had an hour to kill and she was within walking distance of Bonwit's. No, she would take a cab.

At Bonwit's she bought the sheerest panty hose, St. Laurent pumps, a filmy Givenchy dress that was oh, so expensive, a perfume she had not tried before, but it seemed enticing. She changed in the ladies' room and arranged to have the clothes she came in delivered to the penthouse. She went out and hailed another cab. But in the cab she looked at her watch. It wasn't six yet. She couldn't arrive early!

She decided. She gave the cabby the address of Once Over Lightly. Inside, Nick was still behind the bar. He gave her a glance. "The usual?"

"Yes."

"A little early."

"I want to be escorted home."

"We'll have to stop at the grocery first."

"That will be fun."

Actually they stopped at the grocery, the baker's, the liquor store and the deli. And it *was* fun. Tiny hadn't shopped for groceries in months. And then Nick walked her to his apartment building, on Fifty-second Street off Third Avenue. "It isn't much," he said, fitting his key into the lock, while balancing two bags of groceries in the nook of his other arm.

"I don't care."

His apartment was small, but more than livable: lots of bookshelves crammed with books; posters from old movies on the wall; a rattan bucket chair hanging from the ceiling. Tiny at once seated herself in the chair and began to swing.

"An apéritif, madame?"

"You've been bartender long enough. Show me where the kitchen is, and I'll mix. Oh, I see you're determined. No, Nick, not an apéritif; a dry martini."

While he made the drinks, she swung back and forth. He was really very handsome, in a dark way. She liked his long face and his large brown eyes that could be so introspective. He was graceful too—it was possibly the first trait of his she had noticed. Joel was graceful above all else. She disliked bumbling men. Most men were so clumsy. They spilled drinks. And then they apologized. But they were always sure they could drive your car better than you, and then only drove it faster. Even Joel was that way.

Nick came back with the martinis. "Do you drive?" she asked.

"On occasion. I don't own a car, if that's what you want to know. My wife got that in the marriage settlement."

"You were married?"

"Five years. No children. Are you?"

"No. I've never even been asked."

"A lovely girl like you?"

"That's the reason I've been going to a psychiatrist. No one ever asks me."

"There must be more to it than that."

"What do you mean—'more to it'?"

"Just that. You're an attractive, beautiful woman, You're

37

intelligent, sophisticated. Someone must have proposed marriage."

"There *is* more to it than that. You're right."

"Do you want to tell me?"

"Yes, I think I do."

"Another drink?"

"Yes, if you please."

"The same?"

"Oh, stop being a bartender."

She sipped her second martini. "The basic reason I went to see the doctor is that I'm afraid of men. No one has ever asked me to marry him because I've never encouraged any-one to that extent. A man asks me out for dinner—as you have—and I freeze. I once went to a man's apartment, because I felt I should at least once, and slept the whole night with him without taking off any of my clothes. Or letting him."

"You're in a man's apartment now."

"Can we have dinner? You said we would have."

He flushed. "It will take a little while. Can I fix you another drink?"

"I'm happy with this one."

He had innate dignity. She liked the way his dark hair curled at the back of his neck. She wondered if he knew that she had made up her mind. Long ago. In the doctor's office. Only she hadn't known then it would be him, instead of Harry. Would it hurt? She had always heard that it hurt the first time. She hoped it wouldn't hurt too much.

4

She woke up at dawn, startled by the warmth beside her. Then she remembered. Nick was sleeping deeply. She traced her fingertips through the tangle of hair on his chest, remembering lovingly. Joel would be home now, and worried. She had never before stayed out all night.

She kissed Nick in his most private place, then softly, silently, rose and put on her clothes. She went to the bathroom and ran his comb through her hair. She would be back here again. But when he woke without her, he might be worried. Nonsense! She would see him at the bar. The important thing was to return to Joel. He was the one who would be worried.

She slipped out of the apartment and ran down the stairs to the street. She walked to Third Avenue and hailed a cab. At her building, she had to borrow five dollars from the doorman to pay the cabby. She had left her purse in Nick's place. A Freudian slip if ever there was one! But she would get some money from Joel and pay back the doorman this same day.

At the twentieth floor she was very surprised to see Harry standing in front of the door to the penthouse stairs. A slouching Harry, a Harry looking tired—as if he hadn't slept all night, might even have been standing there all night—a grouchy-looking Harry.

"What are you doing here?"

He took something from his pocket and held it to her face. She tried to scream, to struggle. . . .

3

THE FOLLOWING DAYS

Tiny awoke, lying in bed, the sound of her own scream still in her ears. It had all been a bad dream; the only bit of it that remained was the dreadful headache—she must have drunk too much at Nick's. But she had felt fine when she came home this morning. What time was it? Four-thirty, her wrist watch said. At first she had thought she wasn't wearing it, but then she felt it under the sleeve of her nightgown and had to pull the ruffles back.

She sat up with a start. She had no nightgown with ruffled sleeves! She looked down at herself. She was wearing an old-fashioned flannel nightgown, all white, with ruffles on the sleeves and ruching about the throat. She was also wearing something underneath the nightgown. She tucked up the hem: a full-length white cotton slip. What in God's name?

She jumped out of bed. It was not her bed. Huge, heart-shaped, it had a tufted white-satin comforter and an ornately upholstered backboard, also covered in white satin. She looked around the strange room she had awakened in: it was all white—walls, ceiling, woodwork, even the heavy shag carpet. There was a large full-length mirror on the wall facing the bed and she went over to it to examine herself. She looked as if she had come out of the nineteenth century. The long gown was completely shapeless, did not even hint at the lineaments of her body. The only parts of herself she saw were her head, her hands, her toes. The garment was so long that when she moved she had to be careful not to trip. Why, even her grandmother hadn't worn anything like this, she was sure.

She went to the white vanity and sat on the white upholstered chair, staring at her face. "Where am I?" she whispered. "What has happened to me? What have I gotten myself into? Is it real, or have I flaked out and am I living a waking hallucination? People do that, don't they?"

If she were hallucinating, the thought that that might be her state wouldn't come to her. No, this was real. She had to accept that as a fact. The next thing to do was explore, to find out what else there was to it.

She walked into the bathroom. All white, of course. She opened the medicine cabinet and found its all-white contents: talcum powder and cologne in special containers, soap, a comb and brush—in the medicine cabinet, of all places! In the shower stall there was a rack with two piles of fluffy white towels and face cloths. Maybe if she took a shower, her head would feel better. There had been no aspirin in the medicine cabinet. What was wrong with aspirins? They were white, weren't they?

She opened the bedroom door and found herself in a long hallway lined with three doors. Opening each door in turn, she found a bedroom, done in white, with separate bath. Two were empty. In the third room, the last she came to, she discovered a man's suit hanging in the closet, a suit made of white flannel, and a pair of white patent-leather shoes upon the floor. In one of the drawers of a dresser that lined one wall she found stacks of white oxford shirts, in another white underwear; a third contained white nylon socks and half a dozen white-on-white bow ties, the kind Joel wore with full dress.

Joel! It could only be a joke, his playing one of his elaborate practical jokes, intricate hoaxes that turned out to be truly practical in that invariably he developed them into a television act, yet another fantastically melodramatic illusion. But wasn't he carrying this a bit too far? How much had all this cost him? And where was it? How had she come here?

Back in the room with the heart-shaped bed, she sank down into a heavily upholstered white chair and began to recount to herself everything she had done the previous day, starting from the moment she had left the psychiatrist's office. She had walked to the bar, had drinks with Nick and talked to him. Harry had come in with lipstick on his face. Nick had sent him to the bathroom and he had emerged all flustered and apologetic—really comic. He had disappeared and hadn't come back. She hoped he was all right. He had been so kind and helpful to her last week.

Something stirred faintly in her memory. The presence. Was it here now? If it had been, it seemed to have gone. She had talked with Nick about the presence and he had asked her to have dinner with him. She had been emboldened to agree, and had gone to the hairdresser, then back to the bar, and they had both had such fun shopping together.

She remembered every detail of that night. She remembered hailing a cab, going back to her building, borrowing five dollars from the doorman to pay the cabby, stepping into the elevator. . . .

But she remembered nothing else!

Tiny stood and walked out of the bedroom. She was more than ever sure this was another of Joel's tricks. She recalled the first time he had brought home the Boot. The situation was so similar. She had awakened and looked for her slippers. They weren't there. There was only a single contrivance of iron, open vertically to reveal the spikes inside. She had screamed. He was at her side at once.

"What's the matter?"

"That thing. That iron thing. With the teeth. I'm supposed to put that on to go to the bathroom?"

"Of course not." He handed her the slippers she was used to.

"But I'll put it on eventually?"

"It's a present from me to you. For the show."

"But it will crush my foot."

"Not if you relax, the way Uncle Eddie showed you."

"Do I have to remain a polio victim all my life?"

"No, of course not. It's just a new idea for the act."

Always the act. True, it did bring them in a good living. As Joel said, "Illusion is all I know how to do." But what about herself? There might be other things she could do besides illusion. She was young and healthy. Attractive. Just because she was his stepdaughter, and her mother had died when she was young, tragically, in an auto crash, did that mean she had to go on being the Maiden the rest of her life?

No. This time he had gone too far.

The kitchen was to the left off the hall. All in white, needless to say. A range. A wall oven. A huge refrigerator with a freezer and an automatic defrosting unit. All sorts of appliances—toaster and toaster oven, a blender, an electric skillet. She opened the pantry doors—cans and cans of vegetables and stuff, staples like flour and noodles, sugar. . . . The freezer was crammed with steaks, chops, a couple of roasts—at least *they* weren't white. She was supposed to cook? She had never cooked anything in her life and Joel knew it.

43

She sucked her thumb. Hanging from a hook there was even a starchy white apron.

Tiny ran out of the kitchen to the living room. White sofas in a conversational grouping. A white coffee table with a mirrored top. White carpet. More white upholstered chairs.

She would turn on TV. There was no TV. She would turn on the radio.

There was no radio.

She decided to phone Joel and tell him enough was enough.

There was no telephone.

She had had all she could take of this; she would leave, even in this absurd getup. She went to the door: no doorknob. He didn't want her to leave! More of the act, the illusions she had put up with for too many years. So he was her stepfather—he didn't rule her life!

She looked closely at the door. She saw the slot, about the width of a credit card. She had read about this. She didn't know they had them in operation already.

Well, she would try her credit cards. But she didn't have a purse. That hadn't hit her before. She was really trapped in this absurd place in this preposterous nightgown.

She sat on the sofa.

The thing to do was to think. If there was a credit card sort of thing that opened the door, there was more than one. She had heard that when these were used to open and close apartment locks, they gave them out in pairs. So you always had a pair. Or one for him and one for her.

Where would Joel keep his spare?

She knew at once from experience. She ran to the bedroom that contained the man's clothing. The white suit. The ticket pocket.

There it was.

She ran back to the bedroom she had awakened in and threw open the closet, which she had not as yet inspected. Hanger after hanger of very girlish, old-fashioned clothes. She put on the most girlish, most old-fashioned outfit. Long white stockings. A pair of white Mary Janes.

She ran back to the living room, inserted the plastic card into the lock and let herself out.

Only then did Tiny realize that she was still in her own building. She pressed the up button on the elevator, went to the penthouse floor and up the stairs to the penthouse.

She had to ring the bell, because she had no keys.

Maybe Joel wouldn't be home.

He had better be, with the terrible joke he had played on her!

The door opened at once.

Joel was standing there, a benign look on his face.

"My little girl has had a little adventure?" he asked.

2

As soon as his Tiny had slumped unconscious, Harry had stuffed the chloroform-soaked pad back in his pocket, being careful to avert his head to avoid the anesthetic fumes. He had carried his little girl over his shoulder down the stairs from the iniquitous penthouse, then waited, sweat streaming from him, until the elevator came. He bundled the slumped form inside, being careful not to hurt her in any way, and pressed the button for the nineteenth floor. As soon as the doors opened, he lifted her out, along the hallway to 19M, inserted the card in the door, carried her across the living room to the sofa and gently laid her down.

He checked her pulse. Regular. She was only sleeping. Julio had said that if the chloroform was administered swiftly and lightly, the person would slumber for hours: "A good night's sleep, depending on how tired he is and what a load he has on. And the beauty of it is he won't remember what hit him in the morning."

Harry backed away, appalled at the low-cut dress, the high-heeled shoes. She dressed as Lucille did. Well, no longer. She was home, at last.

He went to Tiny's bedroom and to the closet, where he found a proper nightgown he had bought this past week, then to the bureau drawer for a slip to go underneath it. His child must be decent.

Back in the living room, he undressed the supine body of his daughter with difficulty. He didn't tear any of her clothes, although he wanted to rend them from her. He would save them in his suitcase, to show her at a later date just how low she had sunk before he rescued her. To dress her, he had to lift her unconscious form into a sitting position. Her arm fell laxly about his shoulders; he had to remove it, lift it upright, then the other arm, to get first the slip and then the nightgown over her shoulders and smooth them along her body. He was careful to tie the bows of the ruchings so that they were becoming. His little girl must awake knowing how pretty she was!

He carried her to her bedroom and lowered her carefully on her bed. Then he stood back admiring her, knowing that he shouldn't—but she seemed so innocent, so much really the daughter he had lost. She was, of course, she was!

He forced himself away from the sleeping Tiny, his Sleeping Beauty, shut the door of her room upon her and went to his own room. There, he shaved, and combed his hair, made himself presentable. He examined his watch: six-thirty in the morning. At seven o'clock, the night door-man would be relieved from his shift.

Harry went into the kitchen and prepared a cup of instant

coffee. He lingered over it, checking his watch frequently, until it was ten minutes to seven. Then he rinsed the cup and saucer in the sink and let himself out of the apartment.

As Harry went outside, he nodded to the night doorman. He walked rapidly a dozen feet or so, then flattened himself against the building. When the man came out, would he turn right or left, walk toward the subway or the bus?

Time would tell.

A few minutes later, the doorman emerged from the building, looking different in a trench coat, but Harry recognized him. He had turned west, toward the subway. That made it easier. Harry waited until the man was ten paces ahead, then followed him to the subway station. He followed him down the stairs and through the turnstile until an uptown train came along, and then he pushed him in front of the train.

There were apparently no witnesses.

3

"How could you pull such a trick on me?"

"What do you mean—trick?"

"You know exactly what I mean by a trick!"

Tiny skipped past him into the living room of the penthouse, with its Iron Maiden, rack and all the other props.

Joel, wearing a dressing gown, followed her. He was looking sincerely perplexed, his favorite look after he had played a joke on her.

Tiny began to do a soft-shoe dance in her blouse, skirt and Mary Janes. "She was only a girl in a gilded cage/-Though the world felt her famed and renowned/She had sold her beauty for gold to age/She was only a girl in a gilded cage. . . ."

"Tiny, stop it!"

"Why should I stop it?"

"Because I don't know what you're talking about! And where did you get that outlandish getup? It's right out of Gus Edwards!"

"Correct, Daddy, it's right out of Gus Edwards. And where did I get it? From you!"

Joel sank onto the couch, which stood in the midst of the props. "You could just tell me. You don't have to pantomime it."

"Tell you what?"

"That you want to leave the act."

"That's not the point. That's not what I'm talking about at all. And you know it. You're only using your usual obscurantist tactics."

"What obscurantist tactics?"

"You know. Each time you want to do a new illusion, you can't just tell me about it. You have to set the scene and then put me into it."

"Well, it isn't an illusion if you aren't a participant."

"This time you've gone too far!"

"But I haven't set any scene."

"The hell you haven't! Who do you think put me in all these absurd clothes? Who do you think made me wake up in a television stage set? How the hell much did it cost you? Us? After all, it's my money too."

"I wouldn't know. You were the one who wasn't here when I got back."

"I wasn't here because you planned it that way. I'm going to take a shower and get into some clothes I like—not the ones an old creep like you thinks I should appear in!"

Tiny rushed out of the room. Joel didn't know what to think. He knew she had been on the ragged edge for months, or he wouldn't have approved of her seeing the psychiatrist. He had had a session with the doctor himself, and had been warned that because of her natural tendency to hysteria, as well as her theatrical background, she might well, at times, as the doctor said, "act out."

Was this "acting out"? To come home in such childish regalia? And accuse him of forcing it upon her?

Joel lighted a pipe, something he seldom allowed himself any more. Tiny had had an appointment—an appointment he assumed it had been with her doctor—that had interfered with her going to Baltimore. When Joel came home, she was missing. So he figured she had met a man. Then, late the next afternoon, she came home dressed in a sailor outfit that looked like the twenties, with rolled socks and Mary Janes. And she had immediately accused him of playing a trick on her.

She must be in love.

Oh, well, he had known it would happen sooner or later. But what sort of man?

Ever since her mother's death he had been close to Tiny. Sometimes too close. More than once he had almost allowed himself to approach her as—well, as a man instead of a father. But he had never let himself go that far, although he knew that many of his gifts to her—flowers, perfume, furs, evenings out when they had danced together and then gone for long drives in the park—had been more than fatherly.

It would not have been incest, he told himself. After all, he was only her stepfather. But it would not have been fair to Tiny. She loved him, and if he allowed her natural affection for him as a parental figure to grow into mature passion and sex, he would be erecting an invisible wall between her and the desirable young men she deserved to have relations with, to be courted by and eventually—one of them—to marry.

But despite his scruples, despite his wariness that the man/woman thing not develop between them, Tiny had never been successful at the dating game. Attractive as she was, talented, witty, there remained a little-girl quality about her that kept her from enjoying anything more than the most casual flirtation with a man. She must have finally recognized this lack in herself, and this is why she had come home in that shapeless sailor blouse and floppy skirt, those silly shoes, with that bow in her hair. And when she said he had done this to her, that he had contrived for her to wake up in a television stage set, that he had once again placed her in an illusion that he was designing, was she really saying that her entire life with him after her mother's death had been one illusion after another that he had built around her to protect her from the reality he feared would be too harsh for her? If indeed she was "acting out"—again to use the psychiatrist's term—did it mean that by that absurd costume, the snatch of song she had sung, the parody of a dance, she was enacting her buried resentment of him for keeping her a child, standing between her and the love affairs she would normally have had?

Joel sighed and sucked on his now cold pipe. He dropped it into the ashtray just as Tiny swept into the room, her platinum hair down her back, wearing a low-cut black dress, black stockings and black pumps. She was tugging her largest suitcase. He caught up with her at the door.

"Where are you going?"

"Out."

"When will you be back?"

"I don't know."

"We have a date in Westchester next Tuesday."

"Better cancel it."

"You're leaving the act?"

"I don't know. Keep your fingers crossed."

"Where can I reach you?"

"I don't know, Joel, I don't think I ever want you to reach me, not the way I'm feeling now, not after the abominable thing you did to me."

"What are you talking about?"

"You know very well what I'm talking about."

He tried to put his arms around her, to calm her. She slapped his face and pushed him off. He let her go through the door.

There was nothing else he could do. If she wanted to leave him, leave the act, it was her right. He wondered what "the abominable thing you did to me" could possibly be in her imagination. He remembered again what Dr. Feldman had said to him about Tiny's tendency toward hysteria. Perhaps he should talk to the doctor. He didn't have a very high estimate of the value of psychiatry, but in a crisis like this he didn't see how going to the doctor and asking his advice could do any harm. He wasn't concerned about himself, but he was worried about Tiny. Anything he could do that might help her he would do. He went to the telephone, picked up the directory and found the number of Dr. Morris Feldman on East Fifty-fifth Street. He dialed it at once, and the doctor answered.

"Yes?"

"This is Joel Barrett. I'm the stepfather of one of your patients, Tiny Barrett."

"Yes, I know."

"I think Tiny is going through a crisis. She has left home and may have left the act."

"You would like to see me?"

"Yes. If you can fit me in."

"I have a cancellation at nine tonight."

"I'll see you then. Thank you, doctor."

Joel hung up. He was sweating. His knees shook. Why should he be afraid of meeting Tiny's doctor?

4

She heaved her suitcase out of the cab and gave it to the hatcheck girl. The barber chairs were crowded, but she found one down at the far end of the bar. Nick came over, smiling. "What'll it be, miss?" Then he did a double take. "Tiny, where have you been? I called all day."

Joel hadn't told her that. It all began to fit together. "The usual, Nick. And I want to talk to you."

Nick brought her the Scotch. He bent over so she could speak low.

"I need a place to stay, Nick. For a few days, a week at the outside."

"My place is your place. You know that. As long as you want. You're upset. Something's wrong? But at least you're not weeping."

"No, I'm not weeping, Nick. I'm angry, very angry. But I feel good inside."

"You've taken another step? Does it have to do with the presence?"

"I'll tell you later."

At Nick's apartment, after she had put away her clothes, in the closet and in his bureau drawers among his very masculine things, Tiny went into the living room and found that he had mixed her a superb margarita. The swift burn of the tequila was just right.

"I needed that."

"I knew you did. So you walked out on Joel?"

"Yes. He deserves it."

"Do you want to tell me what happened?"

"Not now. Maybe later. I can tell you this—he played a very dirty, dirty trick on me. That's all I'm ready to say now. But I want you to know that. I want you to know that I'm not being hysterical."

"I never thought you were. Whoever said you were?"

"My psychiatrist. Dr. Feldman says I have a tendency toward hysteria—a tendency to act out my hidden resentments."

"Well, I'm no psychiatrist, but that's not the way it seems to me."

"Thanks."

"You needed that?"

"Yes."

She got quietly smashed on three margaritas, then ate a rare sirloin, tossed salad and baked potato that Nick prepared. After dinner he fixed Irish coffees for them both. It blew her mind.

He was sitting beside her, his arm around her. She was feeling comfortable, at one with him and with herself.

"So you've left him?"

"Yes, I have. I wasn't sure before, but now I am. You make the difference. I'm not making any claims on you—please understand that. But knowing I have a friend, a friend I can trust when I need him—that makes the difference."

"And you're leaving the act?"

"That I can't answer now. I want just to talk now, talk to you, say anything and everything that comes into my head."

"Go ahead."

"I want to talk about the first thing I remember. I think it's the first thing I remember, but I'm not sure. I am sure I remember this, though.

"I was lying in a hospital bed. I was frightened, terrified. But someone was standing beside me, holding my hand. Someone was saying softly, as if she was imploring me, 'I know it hurts, Patricia, but it will be all right. You'll be all better.'

"Patricia. That's my real name. Then mother changed it to Sheila. But they called me Tiny, though, because I was so small. Then later, when I began to grow, to develop, to be tall, the name stuck in a reverse way."

"I see. Who was this person?"

"My mother. That's all I have of that memory. I was three, three and a half—I don't know. But I know from things she told my father—Joel: I'll never call him my father again; don't you let me!—that she had been a singer in a dance band. My real father had deserted us; she would never talk about him. She had to support us somehow, so she got a job with this band. We lived in hotel rooms and when she went to the nightclub or dance hall or university auditorium where the band was playing, she took me along and I stayed backstage in the dressing room. I've a faint memory of that part. I remember being very cold and very lonely."

"How did you come to be in the hospital?"

"Mother said I developed a high fever, so high she was afraid to go on to the next place in the band's chartered bus. The members of the band took up a collection and I went to the hospital. I had polio.

"Mom's money ran out. She took to hanging around the nightclub, picking up guys, making money for the hospital bills that way. That's the way she met my—Joel."

"What did he do?"

"He was a magician, a star act. He was playing in a vaudeville show in this city in Iowa—Des Moines, I think. His assistant had walked out on him. He hired Mom, said he would train her. And he paid my hospital bills and when I was well enough to leave the hospital, but still so crippled that I couldn't walk without braces, he took me to Uncle Eddie.

"Uncle Eddie. He was a friend of Joel's, still is. He and his wife did a high trapeze act, and he was also a contortionist. He taught me to be a contortionist and a trapeze artist."

"Taught a child recovering from polio to be a contortionist?"

"That's right. Those were the days before the Salk vaccine, just before. The only method they had was Sister Kenny's—hot bandages and rubs. Very painful. I suppose Uncle Eddie did much the same thing, but he let me watch him practice on the trapeze and the mats. He promised me I'd be just as good as he was someday. See!"

She leaped from the couch, straight up in the confined space, came down on the floor in reverse on her hands and walked on them over to Nick and, still balancing on her hands, bent her thighs and legs forward and embraced him with them. Then she slowly raised herself by the back muscles of her legs and thighs and slid down into his lap.

"See, I'm an acrobat, too."

"Marvelous. If you weren't sitting on my hands, I'd applaud."

"I can fix that." She hopped off his lap onto the couch, while he clapped loudly. "Mom died in a car accident when I was fourteen. I think she was out with another man."

"Oh."

"I had to become the magician's assistant. And I've been that ever since. You can't do straight magic—illusions like sawing a woman in half or taking a rabbit out of a hat or making an elephant disappear—you can't do that any more in this time of glitter rock and the other sensations. It's got to be gruesome. Sure, they still like the magic, they're still thrilled by knowing it can't happen but it does happen, that I can't possibly withstand enclosure in the Iron Maiden and yet come out of it bloody but alive—and be there next week at the same old stand. But without the illusion of blood and guts, they stay home in droves."

"The cult of violence?"

"I guess you could call it that. Joel fought it. He said it wasn't 'clean entertainment.' It was my idea, but he fought it."

"He accepted it finally?"

"He had no choice. We wouldn't have had bookings otherwise. But all the illusions are his. Every one. Believe me. I'd come home and there would be a new setup in the living room, a new torture device for me to be incarcerated in, impaled in, torn to pieces by. And then he would teach me how to do it. How I could get out of it alive. But it was always very safe, with him there to teach me, after what Uncle Eddie and Aunt Molly showed me. Now, though, I don't know."

"What don't you know? The 'presence'?"

Tiny took his hand, drew him close to her, kissed him gently on the lips. "Don't ask me to tell you now. Go to bed with me now. But in the dark. I need you. But in the dark, please."

Nick was gentle with her in the darkened room, gentler even than he had been before. There was a someone lurking somewhere in Tiny that he sensed and respected. Though as she began to respond to him, as he began to caress her further, she cried out, not in ecstasy, but with deep anxiety.

"Don't, please, don't! Don't touch me there. It's an abomination!"

He had gone on, of course, aware of her unexpected lack

of pubic hair, gone on deep into her, delving, satisfying her. At climax, she threw her arms around him. "I love you! I love you!"

"Let's leave love out of it yet. We're good for each other," he said.

"I left your apartment. You were sleeping so sweetly. I kissed you once, then left."

"And then?"

"I went down the stairs and hailed a cab. I gave the cabby the address of my building. I had quite forgot I'd left my purse in your place."

"Little fool."

"So I asked the doorman to lend me money; I'd pay him back. I've done that before."

"And then?"

"I got in the elevator. That's all I remember. Until . . . "

"Until when?"

"The next morning. No, it wasn't morning when I came home. It was afternoon. This past afternoon. Four-thirty."

"What happened?"

"I awoke on a white, heart-shaped bed. Everything in the room, the whole apartment, was white. I know now that Joel was setting up an illusion for me. But I didn't know it then. I was wearing a white flannel nightgown, and a slip underneath. None of my own clothes were there."

"What did you do?"

"I began to explore the apartment. All white. Everything white. Three other bedrooms. Two unoccupied. One with Joel's things in it. My closet filled with silly, old-fashioned clothes."

"Then what did you do?"

"I explored the apartment further. The living room. No

57

TV. No telephone. No knob on the door. I was trapped. I went back to Joel's bedroom."

"How did you know it was his bedroom?"

"His things were there. All in white. White dress shirts. White ties, White socks. Even a white suit in the closet, the sort of thing they wear now instead of a full-dress suit sometimes, with white satin lapels. I knew where he would keep the card that operated the door."

"I don't understand."

"I told you that there were no knobs on the door, didn't I?"

"Yes, I think you did."

"But there was a slit, a thin slit. I'd heard of this before. A kind of credit card replaces the key. Only you, and whoever you give the credit card to, can open it. But if you have the card, you put it in and—zing!—you're out."

"So what did you do?"

"I looked in the ticket pocket of that fancy suit of Joel's —I know where he keeps his valuables that no one else is to see—and I found the duplicate card. I went to the closet where all these absurd outfits were stored, which I expect he wants me to use in the next illusion—but I won't! I won't!—and I found a sailor blouse and skirt, a costume right out of the twenties, and some knee-length white socks. I didn't look for the Mary Pickford wig, but I'm sure I'd have found it. There were some Mary Jane shoes, and I put everything on and went home."

"So what happened?"

"Joel was waiting for me at the door, pretending to be surprised at my getup. I let him have it. I told him I knew what he was up to, that he was planning another illusion without—once again—letting me know. What I didn't tell him was that I was afraid this time—for the first time—of that illusion."

"But why, Tiny?"

"As I was talking, I felt the presence, Nick."

"Again?"

"Right in my own home."

"What did you do?"

"I went into the bathroom to take a shower and put on some of my own things—not that foolish old-fashioned stuff. It's then, under the shower, that I discovered he had shaved me, he had shaved me, to complete the perfection of one of his illusions—God knows that! This man I've lived with all these years, who had looked upon me, he said, as his daughter—who I had loved as a father—he had shaved me to make me look like a French whore!"

She collapsed in Nick's arms, sobbing.

Nick held and cosseted her through the night. When she awoke trembling, he made love to her. Again and again. And each time she responded. How the hell, he wondered, had he managed to tangle with so sun-struck, so fey a one? He guessed he had the knack. But she was really very sweet. Whatever "really" meant.

In the morning, while he was still sleeping, she was suddenly awake, pummeling his arm.

"What's the matter?"

"I know you don't believe me!"

"What?"

"Just as he didn't believe me!"

"Who?"

"Joel."

"Believe you about what?"

"About the television stage set, the clothes, my awaking there—the illusion."

Nick's mind was slowly clearing from the haze of sleep. "Are you telling me that what you told me last night might be all some of your imagining?" he asked.

"Well, I'm same, aren't I, if I think it might be?"

"*Same?*"

"Did I say 'same'? I meant 'sane.' "

He knew he had to choose his words carefully. "You think you may not be sane?"

"But if I think that, I am, isn't that so?"

"The thought had crossed my mind. Not that I think you're insane—don't get me wrong—but that just, well, the pressures of everything, whatever they are—from my limited point of view: your coming weeping to the bar, you know?—might have made you, just for the moment, a little crackers."

She slapped his face. Then she jumped from the bed and ran to where she had thrown her clothes. She dug for her purse, found it, jammed her hands into it, began to spill things out, until at last she found what she wanted.

She ran to him, breasts bobbing, a card in her teeth. "Here," she said. "This is how I got out of Joel's damned place! That's in my imagination?"

She plucked the card from her teeth and handed it to him.

It was a BankAmericard. Unsigned.

5

Joel decided to walk to the doctor's office. It wasn't that far. A brownstone building converted into doctors' suites, it was just what you'd expect. It wasn't as if he hadn't been here before, but that first time, when he had come to talk to the psychiatrist about Tiny, he hadn't felt so nervous. Now he was coming to this man for advice, for help; he should let his mind ride. But I don't want to let my mind ride. Why?

He walked around the block. He had to face it, he was afraid to go into that building, afraid to take the chance. But what chance?

Having circled the block, he climbed the stairs resolutely and opened the door.

The doctor admitted Joel to the inner office and settled himself at his desk, a small, rotund, man with a benign smile. Joel slumped in a chair opposite him. "I have to admit I was afraid to come here," he said. "I walked around the block."

"But why?"

"Exactly what I've been asking myself. I'm not afraid of you."

"Of course not. But are you afraid of the authority I represent, or, possibly, the authority you may think you have lost?"

"What do you mean?"

"When you talked with me on the phone this afternoon, you said you believed your stepdaughter to be in a crisis."

"Yes."

"You said that she had left home and that you thought she might be leaving the act."

"Yes."

"Certainly this represents a loss of authority on your part —as her stepfather, her mentor."

"Now I think I see what you mean, doctor. But there is more to it than that. I could have told you more on the telephone, but I thought the thing to do at that point was to establish contact, not to try to tell the whole story at once."

"I wish others had your wisdom. The telephone should be used as a telegraph only."

"It began last week, after she returned from her visit with you. We had a booking in Baltimore for yesterday. She refused to go—something she had never done before. She said she had an appointment she couldn't break. I believe it was with you."

"I saw her yesterday. But that may not have been the appointment she was unwilling to break."

"You mean . . . you mean it may have been a date with a man—another man?"

"I don't know, but I wouldn't consider it unlikely. Is that shocking to you?"

"No. When I came home early this morning, and she wasn't there, I considered the possibility."

"When did she come home?"

"Late this afternoon. That's really why I'm here. She came in wearing a sailor outfit, a blouse and skirt, such as schoolgirls wore in the twenties—even Mary Jane shoes. She was angry. She claimed I had done it to her."

"Done what to her?"

"She said I had put her into a setting for a television act, where she said she woke up—that I had taken her clothes and left her the ones she was wearing. I couldn't get her to talk sensibly. She stormed out of the living room into her own room and came back later dressed in a slinky black cocktail dress, very low cut, carrying a large suitcase. She accused me of having done an abominable thing to her. Then she said she was leaving. I asked her how long and where she was going. She said she didn't know. I tried to console her. She slapped me. So I let her go."

"Tiny isn't your natural daughter, is she, Mr. Barrett?"

"I explained that before, I believe. She isn't even formally adopted, though I've always cared for her as my own child and regard her as such. I met her mother and herself, destitute, the child running a high fever. I've taken care of her ever since."

"Has it ever occurred to you to make love to her?"

"Only this afternoon. But I'd never do that."

"Why not?"

"It would be a kind of incest."

"Do you think she has ever wanted you to make love to her?"

"I'm sure not. I'm her father, the only father she has ever had; she never knew her real father. . . ."

"But it has been in your mind?"

"That's really why I'm here. I don't care if she leaves the act. I don't care if she leaves me—

"But you do care. You just said you did."

"Did I?"

6

Harry would have liked to stay with his face resting on Lucille's warm brown belly, but he knew it was late in the afternoon and he should be going back to the apartment—to his Tiny.

He stood and went to the bathroom, took a quick shower. He came back into Lucille's bedroom and began to dress.

"Where d'yuh think you're going?"

"I've an appointment."

"I had appointments all day—business appointments—and I broke them for you. Now that you've had your pleasure, you're walking out on me!"

He reached into his wallet, gave her a couple of hundred-dollar bills. She threw her arms around him.

"I'll give you a call tomorrow," he said.

He was whistling, something he seldom indulged in, as he fitted the card—the "key" to Apartment 19M—into the slot. Where would Tiny be? In the kitchen, preparing dinner, he hoped.

But she wasn't in the kitchen.

She wasn't in the bedroom.

Or the bathroom.

She was nowhere in the apartment.

Her nightdress was crumpled on the bed.

There was no sign of her.

She was gone.

The Devil must have taken her!

7

Joel came back from his consultation with the doctor feeling much better. He thought that he was beginning to understand himself in a way he hadn't before. His feelings toward Tiny were, if carnal, natural, and there was the possibility that they might even be reciprocated by her. He had no reason to feel guilty about it. Although he had functioned as her father through the years, he was not her father. He was, in fact, possibly the most eligible man.

He let himself into the darkened penthouse and then went through the rooms, turning on all the lights. Dr. Feldman had thought Tiny's appearing in a little girl's costume had actually been a test of his own feelings toward her. "She may be saying to you, 'Why are you hiding how you really want to be with me? Must I go on, all the rest of my life, pretending to be a little girl to you—I who am a grown woman?' " That, the doctor had suggested, might be the abominable thing she had accused him of having done to her.

In his bedroom, Joel went to his wardrobe. He took out the Mephistopheles costume he had received only that afternoon. One of the reasons he had been startled by Tiny's sudden appearance in the sailor outfit that afternoon, and by her accusation that he had plotted to have her awaken in a television set in such attire, was that it had not been too far from the truth. He *had* been planning another illusion —Mephistopheles and the Maiden. He had not yet worked out all the details, but he knew he would be Satan, which is why he had ordered the suit, and he had pictured Tiny in a flowing gown of purest white. But beyond that he had not worked out the scene, the props, the effects.

He decided to try on the costume and apply his most devilish stage make-up. If the psychiatrist was right, Tiny would be coming home soon, contrite, looking for his acceptance. He glanced at himself in the mirror: he made a stunning Devil, even without make-up! He went into his bathroom, put on the false mustache, the rouge, the padding that elongated his cheeks; he smoothed his hair, painted in a widow's peak. . . .

There was a hammering at the door.

She must have lost her keys again.

Joel rushed to the door and opened it. A middle-sized, middle-aged man in as complete a tantrum as Joel had ever seen on stage or screen, let alone in real life, stood trembling and fuming on his threshold. "You *are* the Devil!"

"Yes, for the nonce I am. And whom have I the pleasure of addressing?"

"Even now you speak of pleasure, you fiend!"

"Even now?" There was something about this ludicrous man that made Joel fall back.

"After all these years that you have tormented her, had your pleasure with her—even *now* you speak of it!"

Then the man did a strange thing. He sighed. "But you are Mephistopheles, of course. And I cannot kill you. But I can belabor you, you fiend."

The man ran at Joel, then away from him. He began to topple things. Lamps. Chairs. Joel looked for something with which to subdue him. He picked up the Boot and hurled it—but missed. The man came at him swinging. Joel ran to the kitchen for a knife. Almost there, he felt a blow between his ears and lost consciousness. . . .

8

Tiny bent down and lightly kissed Nick on the forehead while he slept; then she placed the note she had written, telling him she would be back shortly and not to be concerned, on the other pillow, where he would find it when he awakened. Quietly she let herself out of the apartment, and down on the street, hailed a taxi.

She hadn't awakened Nick because she had realized while they talked that he was going to demand to go with her to 19M, and that would lead to a confrontation with Joel, which she wanted at all costs to avoid. But as she had lain beside her lover, sleepless, she had faced the fact that a confrontation with Joel was essential—in the absurd apartment with the closetful of preposterously girlish clothes. There was no other way she could destroy his pretense that he had not furnished that apartment and bought that wardrobe as the foundation for another of his illusions. He was no doubt inventing a new series for next season and the apartment would be the set and the clothes for costumes; this way he could justify the expense. But he would have to see that if she was to continue in the act, he'd have to accept her as the woman she now was, a full-fledged partner to be consulted before any important move was made or decision taken. She was not going to let him continue to thrust roles upon her, as he had increasingly done in the last few years. After all, it had been her idea to modernize the act with horror effects; she should have a say in this new project.

He must think he really had something this time, though, or he wouldn't have gone to such lengths to assure secrecy and privacy. He had in the past been a little inclined to be paranoid about his illusions, and there had in fact been times when competitors had attempted to imitate one or another effect—but never successfully. But to go to the extent of a computerized lock on the door—who had ever heard of such a thing?

There was a new night doorman, who did not recognize her, and she had to show him identification. Then he was very polite and held the door wide for her. Leaving the elevator on the nineteenth floor, Tiny took the key card from her purse and slipped it into the slot. The door opened noiselessly. The lights were on in the apartment: Joel must be waiting for her.

But the man who rose to meet her was not Joel. It was Harry.

9

When Dr. Morris Feldman arrived at his office Monday morning, Joel Barrett was waiting for him.

"You wanted to see me, Mr. Barrett?" Dr. Feldman asked as he unlocked the door.

"Yes, if you don't mind."

"It's about your daughter?"

"Yes, and about myself."

"Come in." Barrett—Joel, that was his name, The Devil —was self-contained, but under his composure Morris Feldman sensed frustrated anger. After he sat on the couch across from the psychiatrist's desk, the bruise on his forehead was visible. "You've hurt yourself?"

"I was attacked Saturday night."

"Where?"

"In my home—the penthouse. I heard this hammering on the door. I thought Tiny had returned. . . ."

"She hasn't returned yet?"

"No. I was trying on a new costume—"

"A new costume?"

"That of Mephistopheles."

"The Devil? It would fit the act."

"Yes. Well, this man lunged in. He went berserk. He began to overturn things, furniture. . . . He beat me up."

"I think this is a police matter, Mr. Barrett."

"You think I should call the police?"

"Yes." Morris Feldman was thinking of that patient of his, a chief inspector, no less, the constipated one. . . .

4

IN THE NURSERY

Harry looked different somehow. For one thing, he was dressed all in white—in a beautifully tailored suit with white satin lapels. It was the suit she had found hanging in the closet—from which she had snatched the key card! But there was something about his face, flushed, suffused with blood, as if he had just undergone violent physical exertion, or had had some kind of attack.

Tiny rushed toward him. "Are you all right?"

"I'm fine, but are you all right?"

He had pushed her away, as if she were a chair or some other obstacle in his path. "You have been a naughty girl."

How could he know? She sensed that he was very angry —with her? But how could that be? She had done nothing to him.

"You expect to be chastised, and then everything will be all right. Just the way it was when you were little. Well, Tiny, I'm not about to spank you. You're too old a girl for that. But I must ask you to go to your room. And stay there until I tell you that you may come out. And when you come out, come out in the proper clothes I've provided for you —not in those devilish rags."

"Who the hell do you think you're talking to?"

"The man who rescued you from the Devil himself. Your father—the man you were stolen from more than twenty years ago, who has spent all this time finding you—Harry Barratt!"

"Harry, you're insane! And I thought you were so nice."

"Go to your room, daughter. But first give me the key."

Tiny glanced down at her hand. She was still holding the key card. She had been so surprised to find Harry, not Joel, in 19M that she had forgotten to put it back in her purse.

"I won't!" she cried, teeth clenched.

Harry sprang toward her and wrenched the key card and the purse from her grasp. He threw them over his shoulder, far beyond her reach. She shrank back. He threw his arm around her waist and hugged her tightly while tugging at the décolletage of her black satin dress. He didn't hurt her, but she heard the tearing sound of the cloth as he ripped the dress off her, felt herself lifted as he peeled off her pumps, stripped off her panty hose.

He was panting. "I said I wouldn't chastise you. But I must. I've rescued you from the Devil, but you were his consort. I'll not allow that! I wouldn't be able to hold up my head against the shame—I'd have to bend it down if I allowed that!"

He carried her to the white sofa and threw her across his lap. She tried to struggle loose but he held her firmly. When at last she gave in, a memory of some other time, some other place, stirring in her mind—a foreknowledge that it was best to give in, to submit—he began to flail at her naked buttocks until she cried aloud with the pain, the humiliation.

When he relented, she lay whimpering across his lap.

"I didn't want to have to do that," he said.

She couldn't stop her weeping. She hated him, hated him, and hated herself for having given in.

"Now go to your room. I'll let you out when it's time for you to prepare breakfast."

Tiny rose and began to limp toward the bedroom.

"Tiny, what do you say? You haven't forgotten what you have to say as an obedient daughter?"

"What are you talking about?"

"I taught you when you were a tiny child what to say when I'd had to chastise you, much against my desire, but for your own good. Have you consorted with the Devil so long that you don't remember?"

"I don't know what you're talking about, Harry."

"I'm not 'Harry'—you call me 'Father.' "

"But you're not my father."

"Do you want to be chastised again?"

"No. I've done nothing wrong."

"You have consorted with the Devil. You have allowed him to do vicious things to you."

"What do you think you just did, you old goat? Who ripped off my dress, my underthings? Who beat me? Who somehow got me into this decadent mess of an apartment? Who bought me all those silly clothes? Who, when I was unconscious—I must have been—did this abominable thing to me?"

Tiny spread her legs to reveal her shaven pubic area.

"But you're my little girl, my long-lost darling. You should be that way—you shouldn't be open to men."

"If I'm your long-lost darling, you're a dirty old pervert!" Tiny took three long paces forward and dealt him a karate chop aimed at the back of the neck. She missed. He had slipped away, agile as an eel. He was behind her. She swiveled, but not in time. He had slipped something that felt coarse over her head, about her body, her arms, was lacing it. A strait jacket.

White, of course.

It isn't pleasant to lie in bed in a strait jacket. Tiny found she could flop over from one side to the other only with much difficulty—and as soon as she had lain in one position for any length of time her muscles and tendons ached and she would have to manage to flop over again.

Her real torment wasn't physical. It didn't even come from the anxiety she felt about her state of imprisonment. She felt such a damn fool: to have maligned Joel, to have shaken off Nick's honest doubts—but especially not to have understood Harry for what he was from the very first.

It seemed so clear to her—now, possibly too late. Oh, it couldn't be too late! She would get herself out of this predicament somehow. But she felt humiliated, not because of the spanking—though that was bad enough—but because she had allowed herself to be trapped by a dirty old man in such a classic way. She had thought of the apartment all along as a pretentious stage set of Joel's, never for a moment considering the possibility that it might be a trap for her. But it had been, and was.

The man was psychotic—that was clear. All his maunderings about his long-lost little girl, his lost darling. He had a thing for making it with young women who pretended to be his daughters. And she, like a fool, had fallen for it.

Well, after being a virgin all these years—and worrying about it enough to see a psychiatrist—she might as well give in twice in a week. She'd give the old boy his jollies and get him to let her go.

The strait jacket was a discomfort, but given time, no problem. Joel had taught her the muscular relaxation techniques of the yogis; she would just float out.

Then, though, she would have to put on one of those ridiculous costumes and entice Harry to unlock the door.

Once she had done that, the rest ought to be easy.

It took about fifteen minutes, possibly longer (she couldn't see her watch), to ease herself out of the strait jacket. It took much longer than that to choose the least offensive of the dresses, shoes and accessories and put them on. Finally she was ready.

She put her head to the door and cried, "Daddy?"

Silence.

She cried louder, "Daddy! I'm ready to be a good girl!"

Silence.

She shouted. "Daddy!"

No sound.

She began to pound on the door, pounded until her fists hurt, then gave up.

She flung herself down on the bed and began to weep. Tomorrow I'll find a way out. I have to! I just have to!

2

Ambivalence! The ever-changing distance between Good and Evil! One never knew which side one was on—Good or Evil? He knew that tonight he had wrestled with the Devil, had seen him distinctly with all his appurtenances, and had smote him. He was not dead; the Infernal Spirit could never be dead. As witness the return of Tiny. She was still in the Devil's thrall. He had returned to the apartment after his encounter with the Devil, had bathed and cleansed himself from his brutal contact with the Infernal Spirit, had dressed himself all in white, the symbol of purity, and awaited he knew not what—certainly not a reappearance of his long-lost child!

But she had opened the door, appeared!

She had entered the door at the Devil's bidding, with the

one implement that could open that door—which Harry had wrested from her! She had appeared as a vision of Evil, in black, showing her body, but recognizably his child.

Harry went to his bedroom and pulled out the suitcase, the clippings from the newspapers, the photos of his wife at the time it had happened. He compared them to the old snapshot and the clipping in his wallet. The resemblance was unmistakable! This female was his daughter, captured all these years by the Devil, or his embodiment—did it matter?—and carefully reared in Evil.

He had been right to chastise her, as he was right to sequester her in her room, to keep her here in an atmosphere of purity, safeguarded from all Evil. He knew he was right!

Harry went into the kitchen and mixed himself a stiff drink of brandy. He could feel it all coming back, all the horror of the disappearance, that terrible loss. Before he had gone to work that morning in the spring of 1955, after he had left his wife still asleep, as he thought, he had gone into the nursery, where Tiny, a few days more than three years old, lay in her small bed. He had been worried about her. She had been naughty the night before at dinner; sitting at the table, she had willfully kept spilling her milk on the linoleum floor her mother tried so hard to keep clean. Finally he had become enraged; he had seized her from her chair and given her a good thrashing. Even a small child needs to be disciplined at times. Squalling, Tiny had slipped from his grasp, fallen, hit her head upon the still-hot stove. His wife had picked her up, comforted her, put her in bed, singing lullabies to her for an hour or so, and then come back and reassured him that his daughter was all right, but hadn't he had enough to drink?

So he had been worried about Tiny that morning, and before he left for work he had gone into the nursery and picked her up from her bed, feeling her burning hot against his hands, his cheek. He had relived that moment for what seemed an eternity. Had the Devil already taken possession? There was no way to know.

He did know that he had gone back into the bedroom, roused his wife, told her that their child had a fever. She had risen from bed reluctantly—she liked to sleep late—and after following him into the nursery and feeling Tiny's brow, said that it was nothing, only a cold or a sore throat. Tiny would be all right when he came home that night. He remembered her words; he would never forget them: "Small children get these peaking fevers, but they're all right after a few aspirins."

He had gone off to work. He had climbed up and down flights of tenement stairs to wring the money for premiums from people who he knew would never collect the burial money, and if they did would have paid too much for it. He'd worked late and then gone back to the cashier in midtown Manhattan to collect his commissions—$37.50, a good day, but then he might have to pay for a doctor for Tiny and buy medicine.

The small apartment was dark when he reached home. That was strange. Usually all the lights were blazing, even in the rooms that weren't being used. He hadn't been able to persuade his wife to turn off lights in rooms she wasn't occupying. He went through the apartment, turning on lights, calling out his wife's name, his child's.

They weren't there.

He had searched for a note. "I've taken Tiny to the hospital; I'll be back as soon as I can." Something of the kind. He found nothing.

He had known when he left that morning that he should have stayed. Tiny had been ill, desperately ill—he had sensed it. His wife, in her distraction, must have taken her to the hospital, was probably still there, pacing the floors. She had been in too great haste to take the time to leave a note, though she knew she had no way to reach him on his collecting rounds.

Harry sat down and began to call hospitals. First the nearest, then the ones not so near, then every hospital in the book. None of them had cared for or admitted a child named Patricia Barratt.

He had searched the apartment again, had run neighbors' doorbells and asked if they had seen his wife and baby. All the housewives said no, they hadn't, and with the exception of one, shut their doors quickly in his face. That one, the heavy-set woman with the flushed face who had recently been widowed and lived at the end of the hall, said, "No, I didn't see her, but if I had, I'd have wished her Godspeed!"

"What are you saying?"

"She's well off without the likes of you! I wish all of them had her spunk!"

"I don't know what you mean."

"Look, mister, you guys never know until it's too late. And I'm not about to waste any sympathy on your likes. I know you're feeling rough and if you want to come in, I'll give you a drink. But just one drink and no hanky-panky!"

He had thanked her politely, but refused. Despite her crudity, she had at least treated him like a human being, he realized now. What if he had accepted her invitation? After a drink or two would she have let slip valuable information that might have led him to Tiny that night?

He would never know. Instead he had gone around the corner to a bar, had had a few shots with beer chasers and managed to convince himself that when he got back to the apartment Tiny would be home, his wife would be cooking dinner, everything would be all right.

But when he returned it was as dark as before. Once again he turned on all the lights and searched every cranny. No clue.

He went downstairs again and hurried to the police station. He had to wait while the desk sergeant booked a couple of "drunk and disorderlies." Then he told the kindly-seeming man—he must have been a father himself—about the disappearance of his wife and child.

"When did you last see them?"

"This morning, before I left for work."

"Now, when would that have been?"

"About seven-thirty this morning."

The desk sergeant looked up at the clock on the wall. It read a few minutes past nine. "I'd suggest you go back home, listen to the radio, read your newspaper. She'll be back. Or you'll get a call from her."

"But, officer, this has never happened before."

"There's always a first time, son. She's gone home to mother, or to a friend's. You'll hear from her."

"But our baby was sick. She had a fever. I checked all the hospitals—"

"Tell me, did you have a row?"

"The child was naughty last night. I disciplined her. But my wife and I—no."

"Go home and get yourself a good night's sleep. Everything will work out by morning."

"Isn't there anything else you can do?"

"I can refer it to Missing Persons. And I will, if you want to. But they won't take action before seven-thirty tomorrow morning."

"Why not?"

"In this city a person isn't considered missing before twenty-four hours elapse. Go home, son. Do a crossword

77

in the newspaper. Just stay sober so she won't have that to pick on when she shows up."

Harry had followed the desk sergeant's advice. He had gone home and tried to do the crossword.

He had thought to call her mother in upstate New York, but his wife didn't get along with her mother.

At 11 P.M., still no word.

He tried to sleep, but couldn't even shut his eyes. He got up, dressed and went out on the street, this time to another bar, one where pretty hookers hung out.

Billie was there. Black, kinky hair, but with a good shape and a sexy smile. She said she'd stay the night with him for twenty dollars. She was hard up.

Later, she said, "You really took on. Have you been out of the saddle for that long, big boy?"

"Long enough."

She looked at him seriously, then took his face in her hands. "There's more to it than that, ain't there?"

"Yes."

"You want to tell me about it? You don't have to if you don't want to."

Harry had wanted to tell her. He told her everything, even about his chastising Tiny the night before.

"Do you think you hurt the kid?"

"She had a fever this morning."

"Jesus!"

"Any blood, any bruises?"

"No."

"What did your wife say?"

"She said she would be all right."

"Was she angry?"

"No, only slightly irritated that I insisted she get out of bed and look at the baby. Muriel likes to sleep late."

"Jesus!"

"Why do you say that?"

"Maybe I shouldn't be telling you this, and maybe I should. I just don't know. I think she's left you and taken the kid. Now I've said it."

"But why?"

"How should I know? And I can believe that you wouldn't know. A woman plans these things for a long time, she takes her precious time to get every particular down straight—then she just takes off. I know I did."

"But why?"

"Put that question out of your mind, because there ain't necessarily no *why*—not from a man's point of view. A woman just gets tired, that's all."

She felt him lovingly. "Hey, mister, you ain't tired. You want some more nooky. So c'mon. It's the best medicine I can give you."

3

Harry sat in the immaculate white kitchen at the immaculate white table, remembering. He looked at his glass. It was empty. He went to the cupboard, unlocked it—Tiny mustn't see his liquor supply; he didn't want her to become any more corrupted than she was—and filled his glass to the brim.

The next day he had called his supervisor and reported sick. His wife was still missing. His daughter was still missing. He went back to the precinct. Another officer was on duty. He told his story.

"It's not down on the blotter," the man at the desk said. "Are you sure you were here?"

Harry repeated everything he had told the other desk sergeant. "Routine," this man said. "Missing wife. I'll put it through to Missing Persons. You got a photograph?"

Harry handed him the photo in his wallet. The man studied it for a long moment. "Go in the back room—there. A detective will see you in a minute."

"I want the photo back."

"You'll get it back."

"It's the only one I have."

"You'll get it back. Go in there now."

Harry went into the small detectives' room. There was a chart of the precinct on the wall, a calendar, a desk with a beat-up typewriter, two chairs. He sat and waited. And waited.

He lighted a cigarette. There was no ashtray. He stubbed the cigarette out on the floor, as he saw many others had. Three cigarettes later, a young man came in, slightly balding out of a pleasant enough appearance. He stuck a sheet of paper into the typewriter.

"Your name?"

Harry told him.

"Address?"

Harry told him.

"Your wife's name?"

Harry told him.

"Last known address?"

"The same as mine."

"You're sure?"

Harry told him about leaving the apartment the previous morning.

"She was still there?"

"Yes."

"Packed up?"

"No. Not that I could see."

"You didn't look?"

"No. I was concerned for the baby. She had a fever. And I had to get to work."

"You didn't look. They never do. Where d'yuh work?"

Harry told him.

"You been in touch with her family? Her mother? Her father?"

"No. Her father is dead. She doesn't get along with her mother."

"Do you mind if we do?"

"No."

"All right. What's the mother's name and address?"

Harry told him.

The man reached for the phone and dialed Long Distance. "This is Detective Mulroy, Eleventh Precinct. I want the phone number of Madeleine Schumacher, 421 Oneida Road, Mendota, New York. Yeah. Yeah. Put it through, doll. I'll talk to whoever answers. . . ."

"Hello. Mrs. Schumacher? This is Detective Mulroy, calling from New York City. The New York City Police. . . . Yeah, about your daughter. She's done nothing yet—maybe a civil action, depending on the husband. . . . Well, ma'am, she's missing. The kid was sick, he was worried about her, but he had to go to work. He comes home from work, she's gone. Your granddaughter is gone. Naturally, he's worried. We're trying to check out her whereabouts. . . . What? Yeah. She's not with you, then? When did you last see her? . . . Yeah. All right. All right. All right. Thanks, Mrs. Schumacher."

He hung up the phone, pushed it away. "You're right; she doesn't like your wife. Anyway, Muriel isn't with her."

"What did she say . . . at the end?"

"She said, 'Try the bars—any bar. She'll be in one, somewhere, trying to pick up men.'"

"Did she say anything else?"

"Look, mister—and don't blow your top. I want to put it to you gentle."

"What?"

"Your mother-in-law said, 'I kicked her out years ago. She's nothing but a common prostitute.'" He picked up the photo from Harry's wallet, which had been paper-clipped to a sheaf of forms, and scrutinized it at length. He shook his head. "I've seen her on the street pushing the baby buggy, or stroller—I guess it was a stroller. Your kid is cute and sort of towheaded?"

"Yes."

"But I ain't seen her in no bars. Of course, all this her mother says may be so much hogwash. You gotta discount much of what any mother-in-law says. You had any fights with her?"

"I've never met her."

"Yeah. Well, I'll put it through to Missing Persons. This your only photo?"

"Yes."

"Any of the kid?"

"Some baby pictures. None recent."

He handed the photo to Harry. "Get some copies made as fast as you can, then bring them back to me. I'll also let the newsies read the blotter. If they play it up as a kidnapping, it could put some pressure on her. Not for real. All I think you got is a civil action against your wife, unless you can prove she's taken the kid across a state line. But I've said enough—outside my line of duty. Get yourself a lawyer."

4

Harry had followed Detective Mulroy's advice and had a dozen copies made of the photo of Muriel. He'd given half of them to Mulroy and kept the rest. The next step was a lawyer. Where could he get a lawyer? He had never had dealings with lawyers. He decided to call Billie instead.

He woke her up. "Harry, what are you doing, calling me at this time of day? . . . Oh, I know you're worried. I ain't no sorehead. Give me about an hour and come on up."

With an hour to kill, Harry decided to go back to the apartment. His wife might have returned. He knew he was hoping against hope, but he would make one more thorough search of the place and maybe find some clue.

In broad daylight the apartment seemed particularly empty. He found some cosmetics she had left in the medicine cabinet, a book she had been reading from the lending library in the drugstore across the street, some bobby pins, a half-empty pack of cigarettes. Nothing else.

He decided to return the book and pay whatever was owed on it. *Gone With the Wind.* He laughed bitterly. The overdue charge was $1.65. He showed the clerk one of the photographs. "I remember her; she used to come in here with a little girl. But I haven't seen her recently. Not for over a month. You see, our rate is five cents a day, so you can tell from the stamp she borrowed this book thirty-three days ago. You might try Mr. Muller, the pharmacist. He may have seen her." But he didn't even remember her.

Billie had fixed a pot of coffee and some toast and eggs. As Harry wolfed down the food he realized he hadn't eaten since breakfast the previous day. He showed Billie the photograph and told her what the detective had said.

She looked at the photo for a long time before handing it back. "I don't think I've ever seen her. I thought maybe I'd know her, but no luck. But I can get you a lawyer. He's black, but he's good. He's my former brother-in-law, so I know you can trust him. He does all my work for me."

"Your work for you?"

"When I have to go into court—you know—he gets me off, pays my fine."

"You mean he's your pimp?"

"George ain't no pimp. He's my attorney. He's got a perfectly legit practice, with an office and a secretary. But lots of his clients are hustlers like me. I don't know what they pay him, but I give him a hundred dollars a week."

"How could he help find my wife and child?"

"He can show that photo to his clients. Since most of them work this neighborhood, one of them might have seen your wife, can tell him where to look for her. They wouldn't tell a john like you because they don't know you, but they will tell him, knowing he won't report her to the vice cops."

"What's his name?"

"George Jones. He's my former brother-in-law."

"How can I get to see him?"

"I'll call him right now."

GEORGE JONES, COUNSELOR AT LAW was lettered in gilt on the office door. There was only one room inside. The secretary looked up from her typing and asked Harry his name. She was a white woman with gray hair, and looked motherly. "He's expecting you, Mr. Barratt, but he's on the phone, long-distance. Won't you sit down?"

The attorney hung up shortly and came around his desk to shake Harry's hand. He was tall, light-skinned, with closely cropped silvered hair and a firm handshake. "Billie

84

said something about a disappearance?"

"My wife left me and took our child. No note. No trace. The police have referred it to Missing Persons, but the detective said it was probably only a civil action and I should hire a lawyer. Billie thought you might be able to help."

"Tell me the circumstances and I'll see what I can do."

Harry told him the oft-repeated story and produced the photo.

"May I ask some personal questions, Mr. Barratt?"

"Certainly."

"How long have you been married?"

"A little more than three and a half years. The baby came very quickly."

"This is a very personal question. . . ."

"I don't mind."

"Did you have relations with your wife before you were married?"

"Yes. Several times a month for a couple of months."

"Did you take precautions?"

"Every time. But she got pregnant anyway. You know how those things are."

"Has she been pregnant since?"

"No."

"How did you meet your wife, Mr. Barratt?"

"I picked her up in a bar. She took me home that night. It was love at first sight. On our third date, I asked her to marry me. She accepted. We went down to City Hall a month later. I had to find an apartment first."

"I see. Has Billie told you anything about how I'd operate to help you?"

Harry hesitated. Then he said the necessary words as rapidly as he could. "Billie thinks my wife is a prostitute. She says you have clients like herself. If I gave you Muriel's photo, you could show it to your clients, who might know her and where she is. Billie said they would talk to you where they might not talk to me because they'd know that you wouldn't report them to the vice squad."

"That's about it. Tell me, Mr. Barratt, do you think Billie is right about your wife?"

"I don't know. At first I didn't want to believe it. But I have to admit now that it fits."

"If she is, do you want her back?"

"I want Tiny back. I'll do anything to get Tiny back. Then we'll see about my wife."

"Call me in a few days, Mr. Barratt. I might have some news. And leave your name and telephone numbers, home and business, with Miss Casey. I may want to reach you quickly."

"What do I owe you?"

"Nothing until I've done something for you."

Harry called Billie and told her about his interview. "For the first time I feel encouraged."

"I hope it works out for you."

"I won't see you for a few days; I've got to go back to work."

Billie laughed. "So do I, baby."

5

Nothing had happened, though, for months. He had kept phoning George Jones, who was very sympathetic but had found no trace of Muriel and Tiny. The newspapers had publicized the story and had printed Muriel's picture, and some out-of-town papers had picked it up. There had been hundreds of false leads—hysterical people who were sure they had seen Muriel with Tiny—but they had all turned out to be flukes.

Then one evening he returned to the office to find a message that a George Jones wanted him to call him at his office. Harry telephoned Jones at once, but the phone just rang. Jones had undoubtedly gone home; Harry would have to call in the morning. He tried to reach Billie, but she didn't answer her phone, either. He spent the evening pacing the floor of his apartment and drinking beer.

He reached the lawyer at nine-thirty the next morning. "I have news for you. Can you be at my office at five-thirty this evening?"

"Of course. Have you found Tiny?"

"No. But there is a major break in the case."

It was an interminable day. He stopped work about four that afternoon. He tried to reach Billie again. No answer. He had an early dinner, washed down by several whiskeys. He was outside Jones's office building a little after five and spent the rest of the time walking around the block and staring at commuters as they hurried by. He had developed the habit of watching everybody in any crowd: he just might catch a glimpse of Muriel.

The lawyer was alone in his office. He nodded to Harry to sit down beside his desk. He had a tape recorder on his desk. "I have a tape of a conversation between me and a call girl whom I represent very occasionally. That is why it has been so long before I contacted her. She did know Muriel and—well, the tape will speak for itself. You'll notice that the young woman doesn't give her name—for purposes of anonymity, and so as not to incriminate herself. You understand?"

"I understand."

"I'm going to turn on the tape recorder now. It isn't a very long tape. But its contents may prove embarrassing to you. For that reason I'm going to go down the hall to the washroom. I'll be back shortly, but my absence will afford you some privacy. You don't have to shut off the tape; it will turn itself off." He left the office, shutting the door firmly behind him.

The tape began.

"You say you recognize the young woman in the photograph?"

"Yes, that's Muriel. She wouldn't tell me her real last name. Her name in our profession and on the stage is Sally Sayres."

"On the stage?"

"She's a singer. Has a small but nice voice. Never too successful. She often had long times between jobs. Then she'd hang around bars and pick up tricks. Nice kid. A little on the naïve side, though."

"Why do you say that?"

"Well, like for example, a few years back she picks up this john in a bar. She takes him home. He's a very romantic type, if you know what I mean. Sentimental. He takes her for straight—she's a nice person, not at all hardened. She decides not to ask for money. They begin to have dates—dates! Here she could be making a couple of hundred a night, and she's losing time and money making dinner for this slob and holding hands at the movies with him. Then he proposes. She accepts. A couple of months later they City Hall it. Then the next winter she calls me up all excited from the hospital. She's had a baby girl. Well, we had a nice cry together."

"Was she straight after that?"

"From the day they were married until just a couple of months ago, she never looked at another man."

"Then what happened?"

"She woke me up one morning, almost hysterical. She

88

asked if she could bring the baby and shack up with me. She said she couldn't live with her husband any more, she was terrified of him—she was afraid he'd kill her and the baby."

Harry could not sit still and listen to this malevolent, lying nonsense! He began to pace. If this woman wasn't lying, if she wasn't part of the entire scheme, the Devil must have possessed Muriel!

The lawyer's voice on the tape again: "And did she come to live with you?"

"Yes, she did—she and the baby. It was an inconvenience, but I have a large apartment with an extra bedroom. As long as she kept the child and herself to that room during my working hours. What else could I do? She had a cute little girl. I fell in love with the kid."

"Tell me this—were there any signs on the child's body that she might have been harmed?"

"A big weal on her forehead when she first came. Muriel said the father had thrown her against a hot stove the previous night, then pretended the next morning that she only had a fever."

"How long did they stay with you?"

"Not long. A little less than a month. Then Muriel got a job singing with a dance band that was going on a cross-country tour. I got a postcard from her from Pittsburgh. That's all I know."

"She took the child with her?"

"Yes."

"Thank you. You have been very helpful."

The tape clicked off. George Jones came in the door. He must have been standing just outside.

"Mr. Barratt, I checked with booking agents and found the name of the dance band Sally Sayres went on tour with. They are still on tour. I reached the leader of the band in Denver and found that Sally had left the band in Des

Moines. Your child had fallen ill and had to be hospitalized. Her mother stayed with her. Whatever she has done to you —or you have done to her—she *is* responsible to her child."

"You believe all this crap?"

"I have to. I went out to Des Moines and checked it out. Your child was admitted to a hospital there with a diagnosis of polio. She was released only last week. The bill came to something more than $3,800 and it was paid."

"Where is she now?"

"The hospital has no forwarding address. My associate had an operative check passengers on trains and planes out of Des Moines—no results. They're not registered at any hotel or motel. But a student nurse informed him that Sally had said she was going to Chicago after a while."

"What do I do?"

"I think you are at the end of the road, Mr. Barratt. However, you can pay me my retainer and expenses for myself and my operatives." He handed Harry an itemized bill for $2,875.

"I can't pay anything like that. Not on my salary and commissions as an insurance agent. Anyway, you didn't do your job."

"I know you can't as an insurance agent. And you are in no position to reproach me about the quality of my professional services. But you can and will repay me. People who welsh on me do not live long, Mr. Barratt."

"What do you mean?"

"Exactly what I said."

"You're threatening me?"

"It's not an idle threat. I've evidence that if presented to the police could result in charges of criminal negligence against you. However, I believe every man—even a man I actively dislike—deserves a second chance. And there are qualities about you that may prove beneficial to the organization." He handed Harry a card with a telephone number written on it. "Memorize and destroy it. Dial it tonight and ask for Julio. Tell him George sent you. He will put you on the payroll. He will also make you a loan, with which you will repay me—a loan at very high interest. And if you miss a payment, he will have your legs broken."

Harry stumbled out of George Jones's office. He called Julio that night and was a policy runner the next day. He had done well in policy, in loan sharking, as a narcotics courier; now he was into the financial end. Julio and he had even become friends.

Every year he bought a new red Cadillac and toured the country looking for Tiny. He had thought he'd found her scores of times, only to be disappointed. Now he *had* found her—he really had—and he was not going to let her go!

6

Tiny had begun again to pound at her door and scream. Harry poured himself another brandy. He would let her out in the morning, but first she must suffer her full period of chastisement.

If she was to be saved, she must first learn to obey and respect her father.

5

THE DIARY

July 17

My Daddy just brought home to me the nicest surprise! He is such a good Daddy! A girl couldn't ask for a better Daddy!

Last night after I had cooked for him a really good dinner—I had the steak broiled just right, not too rare, sour cream with chives on the baked potato—he even complimented me on the salad dressing—he went into his room and brought out a package wrapped in white tissue paper with a lovely white satin bow.

I said, "For me?"

"For the best little cook in the world—at least tonight," he said.

My heart was all aflutter, pitty-pat, pitty-pat. "May I open it?"

"Of course."

It was a beautiful book bound in white morocco. Stamped in gold on the cover are the words: *My Diary.* The title page has gold scrolls and the words *My Diary* and *By Patricia Barratt*—which I know now is my real, real name—not my other, supposed-to-be-real name, Sheila Barrett. But Daddy still calls me Tiny. I love that.

"Oooh, Daddy!" I jumped up from the table and threw my arms around him and gave him a big wet kiss on the cheek. He flushed deep red and disentangled my arms, but I could see he was pleased.

The diary has a gold hasp on it, a gold lock with a tiny key so I can lock it and keep everything I write in it for my eyes alone. But I won't do that to my nice Daddy. I'll save the key, but I won't use it. My Daddy can see everything I write.

He wants me to write in *My Diary* everything that has happened to me, all the wonderful experiences that I've had, since finally I came home to Daddy. He wants me to write of my education in the Right Way, and how I am at least learning to "steer clear of the Primrose Path to Hell."

Oh, I've been such a naughty girl! I've led such an evil life. Getting up on a stage with hardly any clothes on and letting the Devil do evil things to me. Worse than that, showing myself on television in front of millions of impressionable children and weak-minded adults, enticing them to emulate my Scarlet Ways.

But no more. I am to forswear all that miscreant way of life. In fact, I've promised Daddy that I have already done so. I shall resist temptation. I shall lead the good life. I shall stay home and practice my piano —Daddy has bought me a beautiful baby-grand piano, all in white!—and cook the meals and take care of the apartment for my Daddy. I thank the Good God that at last I am back home, where I should have been all along!

But Daddy says, "You will face temptations even in this wholesome environment. The strait and narrow path is not an easy one to follow. Our animal nature tends to lead us off into the twists and turns of the Evil Way.

"That is why I have given you this diary. In it I want you to write all your experiences since you came back to your own and proper home by stealth, and I had to chastise you."

"But why, Daddy? I don't like to remember those times when I was so bad."

"You are not inherently evil, Tiny, of this I'm convinced. There are unfortunate human beings, though—and you have been one—who become possessed, their very nature seized by the Devil or one of his fiends. This is what happened to you long, long ago, when your mother stole you from me."

"Mother was a fiend?"

"I didn't say your mother was a fiend. Muriel tried to be a good mother. But, as I was telling you, she became possessed."

"She told me her name was Sally."

"That is the name she took when she went on the stage. Her real name was Barratt, Muriel Barratt. But you see already you are questioning me.

If you write this down, write down everything that occurred to you from that first night, you will be able to study it repeatedly, learn the temptations you faced and that you continue to face—and be better able to resist them, to defend your purity."

So I am doing as Daddy wants, what he assures me is the Right Way. I am going back to that first night when I stole into my own home by using a key card I had taken from his pocket. I did not expect him to be here; of course, then I didn't know he was my real Daddy—and he says I'm not to blame myself for this, as it was only a device of the Devil.

I was terribly surprised to see Daddy standing there in the living room. He was very upset; days later he told me that the Devil had tried to take him only a few minutes before. "But I wrestled with him and overthrew his Evil Power." I knew nothing of this then, of course.

Daddy was very angry with me, and righteously so, not only for having taken his key card, but for how I was dressed, the perfume I was wearing, how I defied him. He said he did not want to chastise me, but he had to. Then he took off my clothes and spanked me and made me go to my room to spend the night.

I was very bad that night. I had not as yet realized that everything my dear Daddy made me do was for the best. He had put a restraining garment on me because he was afraid I might have another temper tantrum such as I had frequently had as a little girl. Using the evil arts I had learned on the stage and in the circus, I struggled out of it. Then I began to beat on the door and to scream. I kept it up repeatedly during the night. Dear Daddy ignored me. "I had to teach you your first lesson in discipline," he told me later.

I gave up and fell asleep. Sleep did not come easily: I was possessed by demons that tormented me. But at last I did fall asleep. The next thing I knew, it was morning and dear Daddy was awakening me with a gentle rapping on my door. He told me to take a warm bath, wash my face and hands thoroughly to get the dreadful nail polish off them—this I couldn't do; no matter how hard I scrubbed on my nails, the polish wouldn't come off—comb out my hair, put on the decent clothes he had left in the closet for me and come out and lay the table and cook breakfast.

I did as I was told, dressing myself as quickly as I could—I know today that I took far too long over my ablutions and poor Daddy was dreadfully hungry before I appeared—and came into the kitchen. He had laid the table. He told me he wanted a simple breakfast of eggs sunny side up, home-fried potatoes, toast and coffee. I was to prepare for myself a glass of milk—I detested milk then, which is so good for me, another sign of the Devil's influence—cereal and an orange.

I took entirely too long doing breakfast and Daddy was unhappy about it when at last he sat down to table. Then he saw the polish on my fingernails. He stood up and went to a drawer in the kitchen cabinet, took out a pair of poultry shears, had me hold out my hands while he cut my fingernails. "Finish your breakfast!"

I couldn't drink all my milk or eat all my cereal, although I did cut my orange in half and suck it dry, spitting out the seeds. Daddy didn't like my table manners, but no one had ever taught me how to cut an orange into slices.

"I see I have to chastise you again." I received another spanking. Then Daddy sent me back to my room, after I had done the dishes, telling me that if I was good and quiet, I might come out and have lunch with him, because he would be back home by then.

I admit I was desolate and I wept. I see how wrong I was then. I was too indoctrinated in the Wrong Way to see the Light.

Thank God that I see it now!

Tiny pushed her chair back from the escritoire and dropped her pen upon the blotter. That ought to satisfy the self-righteous son of a bitch, at least for today! Really, she couldn't complain: his gift of the diary and his request that she write out all her "experiences" was the first indication that her strategy was beginning to work.

She had to be careful to put it all down in the little-girl tone of voice that he considered to indicate purity of thought, wholesomeness of behavior. No hint of complaint must seep in or she would be back where she had been a month before. It had to work, if she was to escape from this maniac.

Tiny walked to the picture window and gazed out on the sunny July day and down at all the people—free spirits!— who crowded Fifty-seventh Street. His cunningness to have devised this trap for her! She remembered the time, shortly after she had begun to operate her game plan and really to be able to act it out—as if this were a routine in the act, to be suffered through as you put up with any routine without any real engagement of self—when the window-washers on their electrically operated scaffold had appeared outside this window. She had shouted at them, waved her arms—neither had shown any sign of recognition. In desperation, she had shed her clothes and stood beguilingly in front of the window. They went on washing. She wasn't *that* bad-looking, she knew. Only then did she realize that the windows were of a special glass that you could see out of but not see in through. The window-washers might just as well have been polishing mirrors.

She yawned and went back inside the room to inspect herself in the full-length mirror: Her hair, long without attention from the hairdresser, no longer platinum blond but returning to the color of sun-ripened wheat, caught up behind her head with one of those white satin bows Harry —I beg your pardon, Daddy!—insisted on. Her breasts strapped in by the tightest and most painful of bras—an A cup instead of her customary C. The flowing white organdy dress, high-collared, with long sleeves to cover her bruises, that flowed and flowed to her instep. Possibly adult. But then she glanced down at the white patent Mary Jane sandals and the glimpse of white knee-length stocking. It was disgusting!

After having written all that nonsense in her diary, she needed a drink. She had found where Harry kept the brandy, and how to slip the pantry lock—but she had to be careful not to lower the level more than a couple of fingers a day, or he might discover her tippling. She poured herself a single jolt. Not to have cigarettes was bad enough, but she needed something else if she was to keep up this charade.

She sat at the kitchen table sipping the brandy. In a little while she would have to start preparing the beef bourguignon—beef bourguignon, by God! Then she would toss the salad. Scrape and slice the carrots. Put the frozen Parker House rolls he so loved in the oven. Take the chocolate ice cream out of the freezer and put it into the refrigerator. Set the table. Mix the salad dressing. Check, check, check everything. And have it all "piping hot"—as he insisted—when he rolled in.

First she would regain her sanity. She would go back to what actually happened that first night of her incarceration after she had freed herself from the strait jacket. She had flown into a rage the moment her hands and arms were free. Before that she had been scared out of her wits. Then she saw red, literally. She pounded and kicked at the door, yelled and screamed, thinking that if it didn't bring him, at least it would bring the neighbors and the police. She had no way of knowing then that the apartment was soundproofed.

There had been no response. Exhausted, she had lain on her bed and tried to sleep—but couldn't. That much she had written in the diary was true. But she was still insensately angry. She had gone to the door again—not once, but at least three times more—to pummel, to kick, to scream.

No response.

She had sunk into the bed, feeling that it engulfed her. She would have liked to smother in it. Had she ever felt so helpless? Once, long ago, when she was very small, in the hospital? Or was it before that? When had she felt this all-compelling need to escape, to be anywhere else, and known there was nothing she could do?

She knew she had to calm yourself. That was what she had thought, crazy as it seemed: "She knew she had to calm

97

yourself." What did that mean? Why was she referring to herself as "she" and telling "her" to calm "yourself"? It was an attack on her identity.

Hell, he did more than attack my identity. He attacked *me*.

Who are *you*? Who are you but your identity?

But why does he want to destroy me?

He doesn't want to destroy you. He wants you not as a person, but as a body. A body he can claim for his own purposes. But he wants to make you, as a body, to conform mindlessly to his needs.

That is the attack on my identity?

Yes. You must resist it.

She awoke, hearing the last words. She knew that she must have been talking to herself, talking in her sleep.

She must be in a hysterical state. But how was that possible? She remembered every word. Would a hysteric?

Yes. Hysterics remembered everything. Hysterics never forgot.

And this man, this Harry—he never forgets.

Then he is a hysteric?

He may be paranoid.

But he might be only a hysteric?

Yes. Does it matter? What matters is that you must find a way to escape from him. You must be calm.

And, curiously, she was calm.

She was calm in her mind, but still curiously excited in her body. Muscles in her thighs twitched involuntarily. She felt flushed all over. Something had come over her, and gone, and of that she was glad—yet longed for it to return.

She felt as she had lying beside Nick that afternoon: yet hungry for more.

She sat up, holding the covers to herself. Nick! What must he be thinking? She had left him without a word. He must be worried about her. Would he think she had deserted him? But she had left her clothes. Would he come to find her?

He knew about the apartment. The crazy key card. But she hadn't told him it was Apartment 19M in the same building she lived in. She hadn't let him see the real card, but had substituted her BankAmericard.

She had thought only to protect Joel. How foolish she had been! She had thought it all an egocentric practical joke of Joel's, his way of introducing her to a new illusion for the Maiden series. She had been very angry with him, but she hadn't wanted to harm him—nor had she wanted him to know about Nick; not yet.

She supposed she had really wanted to tell him about Nick when she came back to this damnable place. She had been sure he would be here, that they would have a confrontation, as they had before. Then she would have told him about Nick—taunted him about Nick.

Now neither man knew how to begin to find her! Joel had seen her in Harry's outlandish clothes—which she had accused him of foisting on her. He knew she had awakened in an apartment—no, she had accused him of elaborating a television stage set.

And she had described the television set to Nick. But neither of them knew it was two floors down from the penthouse, in the same building! Nick hadn't been at all sure it wasn't a figment of her imagination—he had almost convinced her of it. That was one of the reasons she had come back here: to prove to Nick that the place really existed, that it was all a trick of Joel's.

Oh, my God, she had been so foolish!

Dr. Feldman . . . What had she told her psychiatrist? About the "presence"? About waking up and finding herself dressed in old-fashioned childish clothes? All Joel's

99

fault. But mostly they had talked about her leaving the act. No, she hadn't told Dr. Feldman about waking up in the apartment; she had seen him Friday morning, before she spent the night with Nick. Had she told the doctor about the presence? She knew she had told Nick. Yes, that was all she had told the doctor—about her refusal to go to Baltimore with Joel.

The presence. Now she understood. The presence was all around her.

Harry was the presence.

How could she escape?

He hammered on her door the next morning. "Get up! Cleanse yourself! Put on decent clothes! Come make me my breakfast!"

All there was to put on was a Girl Scout middy, a pair of bloomers, long stockings and those shoes. He growled at her because she was so late. He said his eggs were "as cold as Bull's-eyes." His potatoes were soggy. He cut her fingernails to the quick with shears. Then he hit her repeatedly and locked her in the room again.

2

July 18

Dear Daddy wasn't too pleased with my first entry in *My Diary*. He said the facts were accurate and I had a certain style, but my handwriting and orthography were terrible. He left in a hurry and came back in a few minutes with a big dictionary. He made me look up the word "orthography." It means spelling. Well, I knew I couldn't spell in the first place. But dear Daddy insisted that this was one of the ways of the Devil, not learning to spell. He had me look up every word he had put a light pencil mark next to—which I could erase easily—and correct the spellings of those words. He had me do it right away, even before I washed the dishes. Tonight we'll do the same thing—but I'm looking up any words I'm unsure of as I write. Maybe there won't be so many mistakes this time.

Daddy enjoyed his dinner, though. He said I am improving as a cook. After he had enjoyed his cigar, I played the piano and he sang—he has a lovely baritone voice. Then he had me go and wash up and put on my nightgown. Then he came into the room, watched while I knelt beside the bed and said the Lord's Prayer. And then he tucked me into bed. He has never done this before. It was so sweet. I felt all comfy and protected, as I never have before. I hope he does it again.

Dear Diary, it was such a good day! I learned so much and, after Daddy kissed me on the cheek, I slept so well.

I'll never be bad again.

Tiny had finished writing in the diary. She had learned one thing from yesterday: the shorter the entry, the less the old goat could find wrong with it, and the less often she would be hit.

She had learned after the first several days that Harry was a complex character. It would be easy to say that he got his kicks pretending that she was his supposedly long-lost little girl and then punishing her. He was a sadist who liked to hurt children, but who got a special kick out of doing it to a grown woman while imagining her to be his little girl.

But it wasn't that easy. Not that all that wasn't true, but he was straight about it. What did she mean by that? Well, she had watched him closely when he had been angered by something she had done that had broken one of his rigid rules. Observing him, she had expected to see a curl of the lip, a hesitation before striking her, that would indicate to her that he had planned it all, had set her up in a situation in which she would be bound to make the mistake that caused his anger and led him to hit her.

Tiny hadn't been able to detect any sign. He meant what he was saying—he really believed every moment of it. When she had come to understand this, her plan had occurred to her. She worked it out this way:

1. Harry had lost a daughter in infancy, or so he believed.

2. Harry honestly believed that she was his daughter, whom he had found after many years of searching.

3. Harry had gathered a large number of odd facts, which he considered to be evidence, that supported his belief that she was the daughter he had been searching for all those many years.

4. Harry rarely talked about her "mother"—the woman who supposedly had spirited her away from him and their home together. Yet he never said anything against her either.

5. Something must have happened between Harry and her "mother" before her "mother" took her away—or this woman stole away the child that Harry insisted she had been.

6. The something that had occurred involved herself, and her well-being.

7. It might have been a domestic quarrel, during which Harry had frightened his wife by severely beating his daughter.

8. Harry was guilty about whatever he had done.

9. All his life he had felt a need to expiate his guilt—wash his dirty hands. But he couldn't do that unless he found his long-lost daughter.

10. Having at last found her—or a substitute for her who suits his needs: myself—he is still trying to avoid his guilt by disciplining me into becoming the ideally pure child he had expected his infant daughter to be in the first place.

So Tiny appraised her captor. Having had him under close observation for at least five weeks, she was pretty sure of her facts. The only reason for compiling the list, however, was to figure out some way she could put her conclusions about him to work in an overall plan that would enable her to escape.

One of the reasons she felt that when he "chastised" her he acted out of guilt more than sexual desire was that though he became very angry, and genuinely so, and hit her frequently—and though he struck her often and hard enough to raise welts—he had as yet to harm her. Everything he had done was within the limits of what any angry parent might do to his child, and feel sorry about afterward—but not feel criminal.

Was he being cautious?

In all this time, since he spanked or slapped her or locked her in her room on the average of at least once a day, wouldn't he at some point have lost his temper and knocked her unconscious?

Possibly he had that first time she found herself in the apartment, when she had foolishly blamed it all on a trick of Joel's. Could he have knocked her out then, or possibly anesthetized her? That would explain why she could remember nothing of what happened after she left the elevator, until she awoke in this damned apartment.

That might all be so; in fact, she felt it probably was all so. But there was something she had touched on in her reasoning about Harry—Daddy! how she loathed the term now!—that she had hurried over but seemed now to be of more importance than all the rest.

What was it?

It had something to do with his guilt. How had she put it to herself? When he "chastised" her he acted out of guilt more than sexual desire. . . .

Sexual desire.

He could be spanking her, slapping her, but never whipping her or really harming her, because he was guilty over what he had once done to his long-lost daughter, maybe even to his wife.

But that didn't mean he didn't have sexual desire for her. Most fathers had for their daughters—she had read enough about Freud to know that, and she couldn't have grown up in show business without seeing plenty of evidence.

Oh, God—the poor bastard wanted to make love to her. That was it.

She wondered what his sex life was like.

It was then that she hit upon her plan.

It was so obvious, so simple, so female. It would work, too. It would take time. But time was one thing she had plenty of—until she somehow escaped from her imprisonment. And the one sure way she could get out of there was if her captor decided that he wanted to let her out.

And how could she manage that—contrive to induce Harry to let her out?

A man will do anything for the woman he loves—as a woman.

Tiny was so pleased with herself that she clapped her hands. Soon after that, she had begun to work on him as subtly and as guilefully as she knew how. She was much more submissive. Where before she had avoided him, had often shrunk away from his touch, now she stood as close as possible to him. She would contrive to bump into him when serving him his breakfast or dinner. When he decided he wanted her to play the piano for him, she wanted to go on after he was tired.

And she kissed him good night every night. And she remembered always to say her prayers.

Lucille caught up with him at the door. "You're leaving?"

"I have to. I have an appointment."

"Don't leave me now. I want you to do that again."

"If I do it again so soon, it may kill you."

"I don't care."

"Well, I have an appointment. I have to go."

"When will you be back?"

"Tomorrow. We'll see."

The air conditioning was off in Julio's office building. It was ninety degrees outside. The two men sat across from each other at the boat-shaped conference table in Julio's office, beads of perspiration flowing down from their brows.

"You will leave tomorrow for Switzerland?" Julio asked.

"Yes."

"You have—I have given you—more than ten million dollars in bearer bonds. You will deposit them in the Zurich account?"

"As I have before."

"I know, but how do you do it?"

"If you knew how I did it, I wouldn't be useful to you."

"You might be more useful to me."

"Julio, we are friends."

"Yes."

"If I told you, I'm sure we would remain friends."

"Yes."

"But if I don't tell you, and the funds are deposited in the numbered account, and I take my usual discount, we are still friends."

"Yes."

"Let's leave it like that."

"It's very hot in here. Let's go downstairs to an air-conditioned bar and have a drink."

"You know I don't drink."

"Have a lemonade."

On the way into the bar, Julio picked up from the newsstand a copy of that day's *New York Post*. He waved it at the bartender, who cringed at the major headline, then as Harry and he sat down together, spread it out. The subsidiary headline was: MAIDEN STILL MISSING; COPS BAMBOOZLED.

"So what do you want?" Julio asked.

"You said a lemonade."

"Harry, come on. I've known you for years."

"I'll have a scotch."

Julio tapped the paper. "What do you think about this snatch of the 'Maiden'?"

"What's there to think? Publicity."

"Yeah. Well, it could be. On the other hand . . ."

"Nothing."

"What do you mean—'Nothing'?"

"What I said. It can only be publicity. There is no other hand."

Julio sighed. "You're probably right. In fact, come to think of it, I'm sure you're right. I guess I'm just a romantic. Even so, some hunch I have—I guess you'd call it that—makes me feel it's for real."

"Have you seen the show?"

"On TV? Every time. The things he does to her, or almost does to her. After all, she gets out of it alive, doesn't she? Almost does to her. Man! They're terrific."

"I don't go for this sensationalism," said Harry.

"That's not what I hear from Lucille," said Julio.

4

July 19

Dear Daddy is going to leave me! He has to go on a business trip. He says it will only take a few days, but I shall be so lonely.

A friend of his will come to stay with me. I don't want a friend of his —I want dear Daddy.

He leaves tomorrow.

Dear Diary, I don't want to confide any more—even in you.

I want to cry.

Tiny left the diary on the coffee table. That ought to please him. She went into the kitchen to baste the chicken she was roasting. Then she poured herself a brandy.

Her plan had been working so well. By gradual stages his real nature was being revealed to her and he was responding to her invitations. Now the timetable was upset. Could this be a conscious choice of his—to introduce a third party into the scene? If it was, did that mean he had seen through her plan, and was countering it?

They had been having dinner the previous night when he had told her. First he had complimented her on the sole. "I am so pleased with your cooking."

"Thank you."

"I am going to have to disappoint you."

"What are you saying, Daddy?"

"I am going to have to leave you."

"Leave me? Why should you leave me? What have I done? Have I been that naughty?"

"It has nothing to do with your naughtiness. I have to go on a business trip."

"A business trip?"

"Sometimes I have to travel on business. I do have to earn a living."

"Why can't you take me along?"

"You would only be bored."

"That's not the real reason!"

"What do you think is the real reason?"

"You don't want me along because you don't want to let me out of here!"

Tiny had pushed back her chair from the table, thrust her hand to her mouth, had run to her room and thrown herself on the bed. She knew she ran the risk of another beating, but this time she thought she would get away with it.

She knew she had succeeded when she heard the water running in the sink; he was doing the dishes. Afterward the apartment was very quiet.

"Daddy?"

"Yes, daughter."

"Come in to me. I need you."

Harry appeared in the doorway of her room. She could see his form dimly by the night light. "What is the matter?"

"I'm afraid to go to sleep."

He came and sat beside her on the bed. "Why are you afraid?"

"Because you're going away. I don't want to be here all alone."

He patted her hand. "You'll be all right. No one can get in here. If you're lonely, you can write in your diary or play the piano. I'll only be gone a few days."

"But I can't go to sleep even now."

"Just be quiet and sleep will come."

"Daddy?"

"Yes, Tiny."

"Will you stay with me until I fall asleep?"

"For a little while."

He had stretched out beside her, fully clothed and on top of the covers. In a few minutes he was asleep himself, and snoring. She let her arm fall across his shoulder. He had not stirred. She had snuggled close to him. He moaned in his sleep, then turned over, moved close to her, put his arm across her belly. Gently she put her hand between their bodies and felt between his thighs. He was responding in a most unfatherly way.

Sighing, she fell asleep herself.

At breakfast, Harry made the announcement. "You're right that you will be lonely in the apartment without me —especially at night."

"I'll be all right."

"I'll have a friend come to stay with you—a woman friend."

Tiny shook her head. "You're only going to be gone a few days."

"It will be better. I'll be home for lunch, and then I'll make the arrangements."

It was almost lunchtime now. Was he bluffing about the woman friend? If he did bring another woman into the apartment, how could he explain her presence? Or did he want two captives?

Tiny knew that if her plan was going to work, she had to have Harry to herself. It would have to work today, before he left on his trip—or not at all.

Tiny went to the bathroom and took a hot bath, so that her skin would be glowing when he came home. She combed out her hair and tied it with a white satin bow. Taking off all her clothes, she put on the nightgown in which she had awakened in this apartment; it must have a special meaning for Harry. Then she went to the living room and stretched out languorously on the sofa.

Harry came in not long after, carrying two large bags of groceries. He nodded to her and went into the kitchen to put them down. "Why isn't lunch ready?" he cried.

"I didn't feel like fixing lunch today," Tiny said.

Harry rushed into the living room. "I will not put up with this insubordination!"

"Oh, yes you will." Tiny turned around to face him, moving her thighs as suggestively as she could under the nightgown.

"I shall have to chastise you again—on the eve of my departure. My plane leaves at seven o'clock, and I thought we would have such a pleasant afternoon together."

"You're not going to chastise me. Never again," Tiny said. "You dirty old man! Have you ever been raped?"

"Raped?"

"I said raped."

"My little girl—the Devil really has you!"

"My little girl, your ass. I'm as much your little girl as the first bitch you meet on the street. You're not my father; I wouldn't have you for a father. You're a dirty old man with an obsession—an obsession I'm not going to play up to any longer."

"I will not take this insolence, daughter." He walked toward her to knock her down, but Tiny swiftly pulled the nightgown over her head and threw its voluminous folds over him, blinding him, and as he struggled to disengage himself, gave him a karate chop against the side of his head. He fell unconscious at her feet.

She pulled him up, sat him, lolling, in a chair. She ran into her bedroom and came back with two more nightgowns, which she quickly twisted into tethers and used to lash him to the back and feet of the chair. Sighing from her exertions, she went to the bathroom to cool herself off, wincing as always at the sight of her shaven pubic area. Oh, well. It would grow out eventually, as soon as she managed to escape from this old jerk.

Back in the living room, she sat on the couch, still naked, waiting for Harry to return to consciousness. It wouldn't take long; she hadn't hit him that hard. He was going to have to accept her as a woman, not as his little girl. He was going to have to understand the crime he had committed against her, and that somehow he was going to have to make amends.

Harry stirred, straightened momentarily, then his head slumped back. The second time he stirred, he made it, kept his head erect, his eyes upon her. "My God, you are as beautiful as you are evil!"

"It's all yours, Daddy-o, if you will let me out of this plush jail."

She walked to where he sat bound and wiggled her hips, thrust her self toward him. "Wouldn't you like a little of *that* rather than going on with this charade?"

"You are more than possessed—you are truly evil!"

Tiny sat upon his lap. His hands were still tied behind him, but he was not struggling to free himself. She could feel him beneath her. She bent to kiss him on the lips, although at first he tried to twist away.

"You want it, Harry. You know you want it!"

"You're not to call me Harry; I'm your father."

"You are not my father, and you know it. Do you have a birth certificate to prove it?"

"She took it."

"Who?"

"Your mother. She took everything when she took you."

Tiny reached under the bindings and opened his trou-

111

sers. She fondled him. "You're a sick old man, but I'll give you what you want if you'll let me go—and never bother me again."

"Yes."

"You will?"

"Yes."

"You promise?"

"Yes. But first you'll have to untie me."

"There's no need for that. I can do it to you as well, or better, than you can do it to me."

Tiny began to pull down his trousers. She heard his wallet fall onto the floor, but ignored it as she tugged at his underwear and pressed herself upon him. When he had entered her, while he was gasping from his effort, she reached down for the wallet and threw it on the couch. He climaxed quickly and was exhausted by the effort. He didn't attempt to hold her, but lay back in the chair, his sides heaving.

Tiny pulled herself away slowly, making sure not to rouse him. She took the key card from his wallet and a few bills. Then she jumped up to run to the bedroom, put on some clothes, go home at last.

"Give me that," a voice said coldly.

Harry was sitting in his chair, disentangled from his makeshift bonds, as self-possessed as ever. Only moments before she had judged him helpless.

"Give me that," he repeated.

She did, handing him the key card and the money.

"You would do even that to avoid the Good Way and return to the Path of Evil."

"You did it too."

"You—the Devil in you—forced it on me. I was raped."

"You wanted it—you've always wanted it."

"I shall not sit here and idly discourse with you on your

evil rationalizations. If you are to be saved, which I doubt is possible, it is going to take much more grievous, stricter discipline. I do not have time to take care of you now; my plane leaves in a few hours. Someone else is going to have to discipline you for me. But I will not be hurting my little girl; I'll be saving her—you. I'll only be driving out the Devil that has taken you!"

For the first time, Tiny knew terror.

6

GIRLS TOGETHER

The air conditioning was on again in Julio's office. It had been very hot outside, even in the taxi. "Just let me sit and relax," Lucille said. "It was a struggle getting here."

"Of course."

She hadn't seen him in his office that many times, but she was impressed as usual by his casualness. The chair was huge for his small, compact, middle-aged body; the desk, with nothing on it but silver-framed photos of the showgirl he had made his wife and their pre-teen-age daughter, failed to achieve the impressiveness aimed at. The book-lined walls were real, though; she could tell by the slipshod way the books were put back on the shelves that Julio read them, and reread them.

"You're looking well, Julio," Lucille said.

Julio shrugged. "I'm looking the same, which is good enough for me. I've known all my life that I'm a fat little wop, and I'll never be different. But I do still enjoy a compliment from a beautiful woman. How's Harry?"

"You've sent him off to Switzerland?"

"Yeah."

"I thought that might be a fantasy, too."

"He's having other fantasies?"

"He thinks this girl he has imprisoned in 19M is his daughter. It seems that years ago his wife ran off from him, taking their baby. He looked for her, he still looks for her —but he says he never found her until this summer. Now he's abducted her and keeps her in that crazy apartment you had me decorate for him."

"Yeah."

"What do you mean—'yeah'?"

"I know all that."

"But if you know all that, what are you doing, having me put up with all his nonsense—especially when the police, and the newspapers, are blowing their tops about the 'mysterious disappearance of the Maiden'?"

"Yeah."

"Harry, you can't just sit there and say 'Yeah.' "

"Yeah."

"Harry, I'm in this up to my ass. A celebrity has been abducted. I know where she is. I designed the apartment where she's being kept. I know who abducted her. I know who's keeping her there in that apartment. And more than that, whenever he calls me, I'm the one who lets him come to my place and goes along with his nonsense. Harry, what the hell is this all about?"

"Tell me, is Harry still impotent? Incidentally, Lucille, my name is Julio."

"I was calling you Harry?"

"For the last five minutes."

"I'm sorry."

"Forget it. Is Harry still impotent?"

"Sometimes."

"You mean what by 'sometimes'?"

"Well, we haven't done the regular thing in a while. Now I have to wear a French maid's uniform and pretend to be afraid of him. He threatens me. I act like I'm terrified. Then he takes down his pants. Afterward I'm supposed to plead with him to do it again. Though sometimes he wants to go to sleep. Then, early in the morning, he may try."

"He's still impotent. The poor bastard."

"I think he's a nut. I don't understand why you let him keep on doing what he's doing."

"What?"

"You know what. He has that girl imprisoned in an apartment that is practically hermetically sealed. There's no way she can communicate with the outer world. He has her dressed in all those old-fashioned, childish clothes. He prattles on about how she is his long-lost child who has become possessed of the Devil. God knows what he plans to do with her sooner or later."

"She may be his daughter."

"You mean it could be for real?"

"Yeah. I've known old Harry for a long time—he's worked for me many years. He did have a daughter, just about the Maiden's age. He had a wife too, a hooker, only he didn't know it. They had some kind of fight—a domestic quarrel. She got the wind up and left him, taking the kid with her. I didn't know him until later, but even when I met him he was all torn up. All he could talk about was this lost kid of his. He's been searching for her ever since. Time and again, he's thought he has found her—only to learn he's mistaken. Now he really thinks he's found her."

"Do you think he has?"

"I don't know for sure. But it fits with what I know."

"So you're going to help him keep her imprisoned, shut off from the world?"

"Yeah."

"But, Julio, why?"

"Harry is off to Switzerland tonight?"

"Yes, but . . . I don't understand."

"Look, Lucille, I'm going to make you king, if you'll make me treasurer."

"What do you want me to do?"

"Whatever Harry wants you to do."

2

Harry was in her apartment when Lucille came home. He was wearing his white suit and didn't seem to be suffering from the near hundred-degree heat.

"Get your clothes off. I want to look at you."

Julio had said to do whatever he wanted. And she had a thousand-dollar bill from Julio in her purse. She could do a lot for that. She stood there, stripping.

"You really aren't bad-looking."

"I seem to suit you."

"I wasn't thinking of myself. But that's an idea. Come over here."

She came and knelt before him. Afterward he said, "Put on the French maid's costume."

"We're doing that again?"

"No, something different. Pack some of your undies and stuff you'll need in a bag."

"You want me to go to Switzerland with you as your French maid?"

"An idea. But no. Just do as I say."

When she came out in the maid's uniform with an overnight bag packed, Lucille saw he was holding a gun on her.

"That's not necessary," she said.

"I'll decide what's necessary. Open the door and stand there until I come out."

She did as she was told. He came out, carrying a long,

117

tightly wrapped package. He rang for the elevator.

"Where are we going?"

"You'll find out. Get in the elevator."

They walked through the lobby. He had parked his fire-engine-red Cadillac right in front of the hotel—illegally. "Won't you get a ticket?" Harry laughed and dug into the jacket pocket of his suit. He came up with a fistful of parking tickets, which he threw into the back seat. He laughed again, stepped on the accelerator and made a crazy U-turn in the middle of Central Park South. They drove a half-dozen blocks to East Fifty-seventh Street, where he parked at a bus stop and dragged her from the car, still carrying his package. She could feel the gun through his coat pocket, jabbing into her ribs.

The doorman spoke to them.

Harry ignored him.

They went up in the elevator to the nineteenth floor. Apartment 19M; of course.

They stopped outside the door. Harry kept the gun in her side. But he handed her the tightly wrapped package. "Undo it. You'll need it."

Lucille loosened the package and withdrew a buggy whip. "What are you giving me this for?"

"You are to discipline my daughter, my daughter the Devil has taken, while I'm away."

"But—"

Harry threw open the door. Tiny stood on the other side, stark naked, her arms, breasts and body bruised and swollen. Harry kicked Lucille so she fell sprawling into the apartment.

The door slammed shut behind them.

3

"What the hell happened to you?" Lucille demanded.

"He beat me again," Tiny said.

"He likes to beat women. He's a nut. But rather lovable. You said 'again'?"

"Almost every day."

"Why do you put up with it? Are you a masochist?"

"I've begun to wonder. But how do I get out? I've tried to escape—it's impossible. And what are you doing here, dressed like that?"

Lucille looked down at her French maid's uniform—low-cut, all black except for the scant lacy white apron around her waist—the black silk stockings and high-heeled shoes. "He likes me like this."

"Then are *you* a masochist?"

"*Touché.*"

The two women examined each other—Tiny nude except for the long, wheat-colored hair that flowed along her shoulders, covering her full breasts to her waist; Lucille ebony black, with pouting lips and long thighs and legs.

"How did he force you to come here?" Tiny asked.

"At gunpoint. How about you?"

"He abducted me. I think he chloroformed me. I was just getting out of the elevator. The next thing I knew I was here, in a bedroom, all my clothes taken away from me. He forced me to dress in ridiculously old-fashioned schoolgirl clothes, prepare his meals; he never lets me out. There's no phone, no television, no key."

"Do you know where you are?"

Tiny nodded.

"You know where you are? Then why haven't you managed to escape?"

"I did once."

"You did? Why are you still here?"

"I came back."

"You came back? For the love of God, why? You know this has been in all the newspapers, on television and radio, for weeks. 'The Disappearance of the Maiden!' At first it was dismissed as a publicity trick. Only after a while has it been taken seriously. Now, though, there's the biggest search on since Patricia Hearst."

"Why haven't they found me?"

"It's just that no one has thought to look for you here." Lucille walked to Tiny, put her arms around her—found that she was cold and trembling—walked her to the white sofa and pulled her down beside her. Then she kissed her gently on the lips.

"Poor baby, why did you come back?"

"I thought it was a trick of Joel's—to persuade me to do a new act on TV."

"Who is Joel?"

"My stepfather. The man who has looked after me all my life."

"The Devil?"

"In the act. Really, he's a wonderful man."

"And who is Harry?"

"He says he's my real father. I think he really believes so. He says he's rescuing me from corruption, teaching me the Right Way instead of the Wrong Way, saving me from the Devil."

Lucille traced her hands softly, gently along Tiny's mottled black-and-blue shoulders and down to her breasts, still reddened from where she had been struck, and her striped buttocks and thighs. "He did this to you recently."

Tiny sobbed. "Only a couple of hours ago."

"It's pretty bad."

"It's the worst yet." Tiny shuddered,

"What's the matter, doll baby?"

"He said . . ."

"He said what?"

"He said that he was bringing you here to discipline me."

Lucille hugged her, then held her off at arms' length. "Is this discipline?"

"I don't know."

"Do you feel better?"

"I don't know."

"Let me leave you, then, leave you to think about me."

The young black woman stood and walked out of the living room, past the kitchen and toward the bedrooms, as if she was familiar with the layout of the apartment.

How could that be? Tiny shivered. She must be, as Harry had said she was, part of Harry's arrangements. What was she in for now?

She heard water running in the bathroom.

She felt very cold.

She ran to the front door of the apartment and pounded on it. Not that it would do any good. It never had. But it gave her something to do.

Then she ran to the kitchen, poured some milk into a saucepan and put it on the stove to warm. She said softly to herself, "Daddy doesn't approve of me drinking coffee, but warm milk is good for me. It soothes my nerves."

She was going crackers, talking to herself as if he were there.

She felt like screaming. But this she wouldn't allow. No screams, Tiny—it's not part of your act.

Tiny had just finished her warm milk when she became aware of a presence. She looked over her shoulder timidly, expecting to see Harry again. Instead she saw the tall black woman whom Harry had shoved into the apartment, the one who wore the maid's uniform—only now she wore nothing. She had taken off her uniform, even the stockings and the high-heeled shoes; she was totally naked—and breathtakingly beautiful.

"Your bath is ready, mademoiselle," she said.

"My bath?"

"More than anything else, baby doll, you need a nice warm bath. C'mon along." She held out her hand.

Timorously at first, Tiny took the proffered hand and allowed herself to be drawn along the hallway to the bathroom. She lowered herself into the tub—the bathwater was of exactly the right depth and warmth—and gained confidence as the woman laved her, first with a washcloth, then with her hands.

"What did you say your name was?"

"Lucille."

"You know Harry?"

"Yes."

"Has he talked to you about me?"

"Yes."

"What did he say?"

"The same things you've been telling me. He thinks you're the long-lost daughter he has been looking for much of his life."

"He really believes this?"

"I think so."

"Am I?"

"Are you?"

"I don't know. Honestly, I don't know. My mother may have run away from my father. The times are right, or almost right. I was in a hospital with polio when Joel met

my mother. Or so I was always told. I know I did have polio.
They didn't know if I'd walk again."

"Joel is—?"

"My stepfather."

"He would know."

"Not necessarily."

"Where is he now?"

"In this building."

"Here!"

"In the penthouse."

"You mean Harry chose this building because you lived
here?"

"I think so. I've had a lot of time to think about it."

"Are you warm and comfy now?"

"Yes."

"Do you want anything to eat?"

"Yes."

"What would you like, baby doll?"

"Could you make me chocolate pudding?"

"I'd love to, baby doll."

Later, in bed, as they lay in each other's arms, sensuously
warm, Tiny asked her new friend and lover, "You seem to
know all about this place. How is that?"

"I designed it for Harry. I'm an interior decorator."

"Did you know it was for me?"

"No. I didn't know what he would do with it. But I decided to find out."

"What did you do? And why?"

"Well, I was curious why anyone like Harry would want
an all-white apartment. In a way, it was an affront to me. As
you know, I'm rather black."

"Not *all* of you."

"Now, you shut your sassy mouth." Lucille put her hand over Tiny's mouth. Tiny nibbled at the flesh of her palm, so delightfully rosy.

"Anyway, the day the apartment was finished, I told all the workmen to go home."

"Yes. And then what did you do?"

"I took off all my clothes and lay down on this bed, and when he came in and found me here . . ."

"Yes?"

"I seduced him. He's been coming to my place ever since, while he has been carrying on with you, telling me every detail of it."

Tiny was silent, motionless awhile; then she pushed Lucille away savagely. "If you knew all this time, why didn't you go to the police, you bitch?"

"Because I didn't know it was you, you bitch! All I thought was that he had some whore in this apartment he was having a fantasy about—until this afternoon. Tell me, what did you do today to make him beat you like that?"

"I raped him," Tiny said.

4

Father Cassidy was about to shut up shop. Never since he had been assigned to the airport chapel, after that unfortunate incident in Flatbush, had he had such a slow day. Not even a Puerto Rican prostitute, or a Venezuelan. And now the long drive back to what he called civilization, his apartment in Queens and his housekeeper's pot roast.

The buzzer sounded. Someone had come in the front door of the chapel. He looked at the telephone; possibly he should call the police. He recalled the time last April when it had been three masked men, who carted off his watch, his billfold and the small sum in the strongbox.

The buzzer again.

No point in being chicken. Growing up in Brooklyn, he hadn't been a three-sewer man for nothing. Plucking up his cassock, Francis Cassidy left his office and entered the reception area of the airport chapel.

A middle-sized, middle-aged man—certainly no one to be afraid of—stood there, his hand on the doorknob, as if about to flee.

"Yes, my son?"

"Can you hear my confession?"

Father Cassidy indicated the chapel's confessional, and gathering up his cassock, hurried behind the newfangled one-way plastic screen. He much preferred the older types, through which a confessor had a chance, if he liked to take it, to peer through the lattice and glimpse his penitent.

He settled himself upon the folding chair. "You have sinned, my son?"

"Yes, Father. Grievously."

"It grieves you, or our Lord?"

"Both, Father."

"What have you done?"

"I have had—I've had sexual relations with a demon."

Another one of those. He should have made him leave, said that hours were over. Too late. He would have to go through with it now.

"A demon who had taken possession of someone near to you?"

"My daughter."

"How did this occur?"

"In the home I had made for her—to purify her."

"To purify her?"

"She has been under the influence of the Devil. She needs to be purified."

"Your daughter?"

"My long-lost daughter. I've just found her—after many years of searching."

Father Cassidy hesitated. During the last confession he had heard, he had brought in a copy of yesterday's *New York Post* to while away the time. There had been a headline on the front page—he had read part of the story. He stooped to pick it up now: MAIDEN STILL MISSING; COPS BAMBOOZLED.

"You are forgiven, my son. One hundred Hail Marys before your plane leaves. And you may leave an offering in the collection box."

"Sure, Father. Here."

A hundred-dollar bill slipped beneath the plastic screen.

"Your flight number, son?"

"I'm not that much of a sucker, padre. But thanks."

Father Cassidy was still fingering the first hundred-dollar bill he had seen in many years when the .38-caliber bullet smashed the plastic screen and entered his cerebrum, ending his life.

5

It was the middle of the night. Lucille had lain awake, thinking. Finally she caressed Tiny into consciousness. "Look, there's one thing that doesn't figure."

"What do you mean?" Tiny asked sleepily.

"If Harry—this guy, whoever he is, some nut or your father or whatever—managed to abduct you right in this building, after having me prepare this apartment for him—understand?—well, he must've met you someplace before, have 'found' you someplace. Right?"

"He did."

"Where was that?"

"At a bar."

"A bar. Oh, my God!" A bar yet. "What were you doing in a bar?"

"Drinking."

"It figures. You go to a bar to drink. But why were you drinking in a bar?"

"I'd just been to my psychiatrist."

"So next you go to a bar?"

"I was weeping."

"So what happened?"

"The bartender was very nice."

"The bartender was very nice?"

"He gave me a paper napkin to dry my eyes."

"How does Harry come into the picture?"

"He was very nice too. He was sitting next to me. He told me about his runaway bride. How in time you get over these things."

"What did that have to do with you?"

"Nothing. Except . . ."

"Except what?"

"I'd just been to my psychiatrist."

"So you'd been to your psychiatrist. What has that to do with it?"

"From talking with him, listening to him, I had finally realized that if I was going to live my life, I was going to have to leave my father—Joel."

"Tiny . . . Joel is your stepfather?"

"Yes."

"He's been the only father you had?"

"Yes."

"Why leave him?"

"It's always the act—the act. I haven't been able to have a life of my own. I was afraid to go out to dinner with a man. Once, more than once, when I did, I ran away. That's why what Harry said to me that day made me think."

"What did he say?" Lucille asked.

"He said—and I hope I'm quoting him right; I didn't understand at first and then I thought and thought about it—he said, 'You can't leave someone about whom your feelings are ambivalent.' "

"Harry said that to you?"

"Yes."

"The son of a bitch!"

"Why do you say that?"

"Don't you see what that says about him—what he's saying about himself?"

"No. I've thought a lot about it—but no." Tiny sighed.

"Let me ask you this—did he say anything else along these lines?"

"He has said again and again, usually before he chastises me, that ambivalence is the ever-changing distance between Good and Evil. He says that I've been caught by the forces of Evil because I'm ambivalent."

"What does he mean? Actually, what's the sense of asking what a nut means?—but I don't get it."

"I didn't either at first. I didn't for a long time. But I think I do now. He sees only one way—one life style, you might say—as being the right way. If you're attracted to living different ways, that's wrong. That's evil."

"He *is* a nut!" Lucille seemed sure of it now.

"But you like him. You've let him . . . make love to you."

"Well, I got things screwed up with me, too."

"The whip he threw in the door?"

"Yeah."

"I don't like being hurt."

"I do."

6

After she had served the second round of champagne on Flight 203 to Zurich, Beth Ann chatted with the other stewardess, Gabrielle, at the canteen. "Have some bubbly. I've two extra."

"Another teetotaler in first-class?"

"The same guy I see once a month. The one who won't take any food and brings on his own bag of groceries."

"Oh, that one. Hey, if I remember right, he doesn't even eat his lobster tail or filet mignon?"

"That's the one."

"May I have lobster tail tonight? I'm on a diet."

"I'd already decided to let you have it."

"Sweet. Hey, what do you think he really has in that grocery bag?"

"I dunno. But that's customs' problem, not ours."

7

Afterward, sweating from her exertion, Tiny flopped down on the bed beside Lucille, who was gasping with pain. "Don't ask me to do that again."

"You were marvelous."

"But I don't want to hurt you again. I don't like hurting people."

"You prefer to be hurt? You want me to do it to you?" Lucille asked.

"No!"

"But he hurts you all the time—on TV."

"You're talking about Joel?"

"Of course. Who else?"

"He has never hurt me. It's all an illusion. My father would never hurt me."

"Tiny, who is your father?"

"I don't know. Oh, I don't *know*. Just get me out of here. Out!"

They slept in each other's arms all night. The next morning, Tiny prepared a warm bath for Lucille and bathed her sore and swollen back. Then she prepared breakfast.

"We *do* have to get out of here," she said.

"But how? Baby doll, I designed this place. It's practically hermetically sealed."

"I know. Tell me, why haven't they found me?"

"They haven't thought of looking here."

"But what about Joel—why hasn't he looked for me?" Tiny was close to crying.

"He's the first one who went to the police."

"The *first* one?" Tiny asked.

"There was another—Nick Cavolla. He said you had left things in his place."

"He's the bartender. I came to him after I thought Daddy —Joel—was playing tricks on me. I stayed with him. Then I came back here."

"You fool!"

"What happened to Nick?"

"He's being held as a material witness. What he told the police he knew about your disappearance caused them to lock him up—for his own protection."

"And Daddy—Joel?"

"The newspapers say they are suspecting he did it."

"My God! They think *he* killed me?"

"Yes."

"I have to get out of here, do you understand? There's something else you know that you're not telling me!"

"There's nothing else I know. Nothing," Lucille said.

8

Harry presented the bearer bonds to the teller at the Swiss bank, who as usual chided him on how tattered they were. But he cashed them, took Harry's deposit slip for Julio's numbered account, gave Harry his change in Swiss francs. Harry presented another deposit slip—this time to his own numbered account. The teller processed it.

The teller wrinkled his nose as he gave back the receipts. "One would think you had wrapped your sandwiches in the bonds," he said.

Harry was already walking off to the taxi stand, on his way to the airport.

9

Later that morning, Lucille remembered the bag Harry had had her pack and which he had thrown in after her when he kicked her sprawling into the apartment. There were lingerie, panty hose and a dress in it, which she gave now to Tiny. Having put them on, Tiny looked at herself in the mirror. "They don't fit, but at least I'll be decent when we get out. . . . How *are* we going to get out?"

"I have an idea," Lucille said. She went to the kitchen and came back with a cast-iron skillet. Tiny hated it because it was so heavy and hard to clean, but Harry had insisted that she fry his eggs in it.

"What are you doing with that?"

"You'll see. Do you have a piece of paper and some string?"

Tiny tore a page from *My Diary* and brought it to Lucille, together with one of her hair ribbons. "Will these do?"

Lucille grimaced. "They'll have to, I guess. . . . Now a pencil or a pen."

Tiny brought the gold-plated ballpoint that dear Daddy had given her with his present of the diary. She handed it to Lucille, who handed it back to her with the page and the ribbon. "Now write a note on it asking for help."

"A note?"

"Something that will bring help."

"But how will that work?"

"You'll see."

Tiny wrote:

Help!
I've been imprisoned in this building—Apartment 19M—for weeks and weeks. I am well, but desperate. Please come to my aid at once.
Tiny (The Maiden)

"Is that all right?"

Lucille read it several times. "Not bad."

"Now what?"

Lucille took her by the hand and led her to one of the picture windows, pulling aside the drapes. She tied the ribbon to the page of the diary, which she had rolled up tightly, and then to the handle of the skillet. "Now throw it as hard as you can out the window."

"You mean break the glass? But we're nineteen stories up. It could kill somebody."

"It's a chance we must take."

"I won't do it. I'm not going to be part of killing an innocent person, even by accident. Why, Lucille, you know how heavy that thing is! If it fell on the skull of somebody walking down there—No—I won't do it."

"Then I will!" Lucille shouted. She grabbed the skillet from Tiny's hands and threw it at the window. It bounced back onto the carpet.

But there was a crack in the glass.

Tiny had seized the skillet, but Lucille came up to her from behind and pulled her back until she was almost doubled over and had to let go of the cast-iron pan. Then Lucille clutched it, ran to the window and began to hammer at the crack.

At first there were only more cracks, then the glass crystallized but still held. Lucille knew from her specifications that it would never shatter, but a hole could be made in it. And at last, after much hammering, there was a jagged hole, through which she threw the skillet.

They ran to the next window, to see what happened. The skillet didn't hit a passer-by. It fell into the middle of East Fifty-seventh Street and was immediately run over by a trailer truck. The next they saw of it, it was deeply embedded in the sticky asphalt of July.

Lucille gasped. Tiny laughed. She ran to the escritoire, picked up the diary, ran back to the window.

"What are you doing?"

"As long as you've made that hole, I'm throwing my diary through it. Maybe someone will pick that up and come to our rescue!"

Lucille watched her do it and then they collapsed hysterically in each other's arms.

Harry returned late that night. Seeing the broken window, he said angrily to Lucille, "I told you to take care of my daughter and discipline her. You have disobeyed me. I shall have to tend to you."

To Tiny, he said, "Take off that whoring garment you

must have been given by this Demon and then come back and prepare my dinner."

Tiny felt a true murderous rage, such as she had never known before. She flung herself upon him, pummeling him. He threw her off as if she were weightless and she found herself doubled up against the piano.

"Go to your room! And do not come out unless you are fully and decently dressed."

Tiny fled to her room. She slammed the door, hearing his footsteps close behind her. Trembling, she placed her ear to the door. He was walking back toward the living room.

She heard a series of screams. Then she heard nothing. Then Lucille said, quietly but desperately, "No, please don't. Please don't do that to me."

"It won't hurt that much. It will even be pleasant before the end."

Lucille began to moan. Once a pet dog of Tiny's had eaten powdered glass given it by neighbors who had hated what it did to their garden. Toto had moaned like that.

Then she heard a long scream—a howl—near at first, then far off, then all was silence.

She began to pound on the door.

It fell open. Harry stood there. "No need for you to do that, daughter. Your father will never hurt you. Chastise you, yes. To show you the Right Way. But you aren't really a bad girl."

He took her by the hand, seeming to ignore the fact that she still wore Lucille's dress. He led her along the hall to the living room, where the lights blazed.

The window, now totally without glass, gaped.

He led her to the sill and made her stand dizzily at the edge, where she felt as if she were about to fall out.

"Look down!"

There, on the street below, lay a broken form. A black form. In a maid's uniform.

"Lucille!"

"That's what happens to really bad girls. Now be a good girl. Put on some decent clothes and . . ."

"And what?"

"I'll go without my dinner. I had the last of my sandwiches on the plane. Yes, I'll go without my dinner, and take you home to Hell."

7

THE SEARCH

Morris Feldman, Dr. Morris Feldman, is taking a walk. Not all the king's horses, nor all the king's men, can put Dr. Morris Feldman together again. Dr. Morris Feldman is taking a walk. "Psychiatry," his father says. "After all these years your mother and I have scrimped and saved only that you should be a doctor, you're going into nut medicine?" Morris Feldman is taking a walk. Without even a thought of Winnie the Pooh. I shall petition the Congress that every psychiatrist, by law, be apportioned a teddy bear. Dr. Morris Feldman is taking a walk. There's no Changing of the Guard. There's no Buckingham Palace. There's no Tigger. Only Morris Feldman taking a walk.

Hell, it was long past midnight. He had listened to the same stuff all day. Each patient thought his contribution "original." And he had listened. And listened. He had listened to Phillip Smith, who was sure that the reason his wife threw out *The New York Times* before he had finished reading it, a week later, was because she wanted to cut him off from the world and "make him her child." "And why haven't you read it after a week?" "I'm too busy responding to her demands for affection." He had listened to Oscar

Troy, who was concerned with the wasteful use of paper bags. "Every time I buy a lemon in a store, they insist on putting it in a paper bag—with a sales slip." So why didn't he refuse the paper bag? "I did, but the next store I went into to buy a cantaloupe insisted on charging me for the lemon." And he had listened to Marian Peters, who worried that her paintings were always dominated by dark blue, though she began with lemon yellows and oranges. "It makes me want to cry." And she had, at forty-five dollars an hour.

Dr. Morris Feldman is taking a walk. Turning onto East Fifty-seventh Street, Dr. Morris Feldman had a big decision to make. A decision of crucial importance: should he go right or left? Left would lead him toward Park Avenue. Right would lead him toward the East River. Either way he was likely to be mugged. He turned right. "To be mugged, or not to be mugged, is that the question?"

A nut doctor. Well, all right. His father had died last year from a broken neck after slipping on a broken stair tread while trying to collect the rent in an apartment he had refused to have repaired. Dr. Morris Feldman is taking a walk. He is walking past a gentleman's resale shop. Just what Dr. Morris Feldman needs—a used gentleman.

He saw the flashing light of a police car a block or so away, heard the *whoop-whoop* of others arriving, quickened his pace. Just what he needed—or the last thing he needed? —a little voyeuristic excitement tonight. And he thought of his patient Inspector Charles Waverly. Or rather *Chief* Inspector Charles Waverly.

Dr. Morris Feldman, while taking his walk, saw Chief Inspector Charles Waverly as he had last seen him, as he would see him again, and again, as steadfast as the Changing of the Guard at Buckingham Palace, his own favorite Tigger, doing—what? Doing absolutely nothing, but star-

137

ing at him with those brown button eyes in that dough-white face with that slack mouth decorated by the wispy, yellowish, kittenish mustache, leaning on his oversize desk, saying, "If this profile you've given me is accurate, or even a rough guide, why haven't we found someone who matches the description? Why don't we have some results?"

Why haven't you looked in the right places, Chief Inspector? Why call me in for advice, after caging the two people who might possibly have helped, Nick and Joel? You knew Nick was the last person to have seen her, the man who had been her lover, the man to whom she had confided her secret doubts about Joel. But she confided similar doubts to me—and I am free, walking the streets. Dr. Morris Feldman is saying his prayers.

Who kidnapped the Maiden? Joel? The man who had been her protector almost her entire life? The man who had volunteered to pay her hospital bill in Iowa, who had made her mother part of his act until she died of an automobile accident in 1966—an accident authenticated by Chief Inspector Waverly himself at God knows what cost to the taxpayers—the man to whom she was essential as his magician's assistant, for he had had to abandon specific parts of his act after her disappearance?

There was an empty soft drink can lying on the sidewalk and Dr. Morris Feldman kicked it. So who had kidnapped Tiny? He had given Chief Inspector Charles Waverly a full profile of the man, not that it had done any good. He remembered well the day at the end of June when dough-faced button-eyed Tigger had called him into his office. Appointments? Break them! This is more important.

Waverly hadn't even offered him a cigarette. He had said, "Dr. Feldman, from this memorandum of yours that you have so kindly given us, I take it we are to look for a—as you put it, if I read you correctly—a 'sociopath'?"

"That's correct."

"And, if I understand you, a sociopath is someone who is determined to test the barriers of society?"

"That is correct."

"He is not necessarily a criminal?"

"That is correct."

"But he may become one?"

"Many go through life without an arrest; others are less fortunate."

"You compare the sociopath to the man who attempts to hijack an airliner."

"Yes."

"Why?"

"Both have a common problem."

"And this problem consists of a search for a lost or mislaid identity, which the sociopath, or hijacker, thinks he will find, or at least reclaim, by means of his criminal act?"

"Yes. But further, this man is desperately trying to call attention to his plight—he is calling for help."

Waverly had snorted, bucked back in his chair like a just-hooked tarpon, and then had jumped up, grabbed Dr. Morris Feldman's neatly bound presentation from his desk and thrown it into the wastebasket. "Nonsense! If that's the only clue you can give, that's what I think of your psychiatry!"

"There are other things in my profile," Feldman had said, holding his temper despite the chief inspector's hysterical behavior.

"What? The man's a sadomasochist? Our prisons are full of them."

"He is also engaged, and has been for some time—possibly most of his lifetime—in some business, profession or activity in which he habitually carries out procedures that either humiliate him or make him feel guilty."

"So is every other criminal in the country. So is Joel Barrett, making a livelihood of intimidating his daughter in public."

"But Joel does not hide his act."

"But his daughter ran away from it."

"You really believe Joel is guilty?"

The chief inspector nodded his head. "He has her imprisoned someplace—God knows where. We've looked just about everywhere, but we'll continue to search until this damnable mess is settled. I only hope we find her alive."

"I can go back to my patients?" Dr. Morris Feldman had asked.

"You can go back to your patients," Chief Inspector Charles Waverly had said. Then he added with a growl, "But keep yourself available in case we need you. This thing isn't over with yet."

Christopher Robin had continued walking along East Fifty-seventh Street as he remembered the chief inspector's words. By now there were many police cars and an ambulance clustered in the middle of the block. If an ambulance was there, they didn't need a doctor's assistance and there was no point in gawking. He could see the tarpaulin-covered figure lying in the middle of the street.

It looked inert.

Feldman turned to go back in the other direction, toward his apartment, when he stumbled on something.

He picked it up.

A book bound in leather, with a gold-plated clasp.

A book entitled *My Diary.*

In the dim street light he glanced at a page or two, recognized the handwriting.

Unmistakably Tiny's! He had seen it only a few times in

notes she had written him about dreams she had had—he encouraged his patients to keep notepaper and a pen or pencil on the bedside table—but it was so distinctive he couldn't be mistaken. The large, childish letters. The capitals that were only slightly larger than the lower case. But more than that, the tendency of each line to run uphill. He was so excited that he could no longer continue his walk. He hailed a cab.

"You know what happened down Fifty-seventh?" the driver asked.

"No. An accident?"

"Some dame threw herself out a window—some black broad. Splattered all over. I was just going past when it happened. She just missed my cab."

"Another suicide."

"Yeah. They get all coked up and they jump."

"What building was it?" Morris Feldman did not really want to know; he was making conversation.

"That tall one—259."

Tiny's address! Could it be? But the cabby had said she was black. "Are you sure she was a Negro?"

"Sure. I seen her with my own eyes, didn't I? What was left of her, I mean. Just as they were covering her up. She was wearing one of those maid's dresses—like you see in the movies."

They had pulled up at Feldman's address. He thrust a couple of dollars through the partition and, clutching the diary, hurried up the steps.

As soon as he reached the study, he began to examine *My Diary*. He saw that the front flyleaf had been torn from it. But the other pages remained, most of them blank, but a few of them covered with Tiny's large handwriting. He read:

My Daddy just brought home to me the nicest surprise! He is such a good Daddy! A girl couldn't ask for a better Daddy!

Last night after I had cooked for him a really good dinner—I had the steak broiled just right, not too rare, sour cream with chives on the baked potato—he even complimented me on the salad dressing—he went into his room and brought out a package wrapped in white tissue paper with a lovely white satin bow.

I said, "For me?"

"For the best little cook in the world—at least tonight," he said.

My heart was all aflutter, pitty-pat, pitty-pat. "May I open it?"

"Of course."

It was a beautiful book bound in white morocco. Stamped in gold on the cover are the words: *My Diary.* The title page has gold scrolls and the words *My Diary* and *By Patricia Barratt*—which I know now is my real, real name—not my other, supposed-to-be-real name, Sheila Barrett. But Daddy still calls me Tiny. I love that.

Dr. Feldman laid the small book on the table, face down. He began to pace. A cry for help! Or was he imagining things? He remembered a ward patient whom others had considered a hopeless schizophrenic; when she began to attempt to communicate with him, she had always addressed him as "My Diary."

But Tiny was a functioning young stage professional, not a hopeless schizophrenic. What was the date of the first entry in *My Diary?* July 17. Five weeks after her disappearance. Could someone have reduced the viable young being he had known so short a time before to this in that time?

Or was she posing—trying to please her captor—and at the same time attempting to communicate, hoping somehow to get the diary to the outside world? Feldman read on.

The diary has a gold hasp on it, a gold lock with a tiny key so I can lock it and keep everything I write in it for my eyes alone. But I won't do that to my nice Daddy. I'll save the key, but I won't use it. My Daddy can see everything I write.

Irony there. Or was it? Dr. Feldman felt he had missed something and went back and reread the continuation of the entry. He *had* missed something! A paragraph preceded what he had just read. It was this pretend child-person's response to the gift.

"Oooh, Daddy!" I jumped up from the table and threw my arms around him and gave him a big wet kiss on the cheek. He flushed deep red and disentangled my arms, but I could see he was pleased.

July 17? Feldman thought back. Joel hadn't been arrested yet, if he remembered correctly. That had taken place only yesterday. But Waverly had already suspected him. What else did the diary say?

He wants me to write in *My Diary* everything that has happened to me, all the wonderful experiences that I've had, since finally I came home to Daddy. He wants me to write of my education in the Right Way, and how I am at least learning to "steer clear of the Primrose Path to Hell."

Oh, I've been such a naughty girl! I've led such an evil life. Getting up on stage with hardly any clothes on and letting the Devil do evil things to me. Worse than that, showing myself on television in front of millions of impressionable children and weak-minded adults, enticing them to emulate my Scarlet Ways.

It was so damned ambiguous.

It could have been Joel who abducted her. Feldman had ignored Waverly's hypothesis all along, because his last interview with Joel had left him convinced that any desires he had for his stepdaughter were only fantasy. But the doctor had noted his puritanical streak—how basically the man detested the act he put on with his daughter, the act which she had suggested in the first place. All the business of her waking up on a new stage set, with no clothes but little-girl costumes. It would fit. Damn it, it would fit!

Dr. Feldman forced himself to read on.

> But no more. I am to forswear all that miscreant way of life. In fact, I've promised Daddy that I have already done so. I shall resist temptation. I shall lead the good life. I shall stay home and practice my piano —Daddy has bought me a beautiful baby-grand piano . . ."

But Tiny had a concert grand at home. Feldman was sure she had told him so! He began to flip and scan pages.

The last entry stopped him. July 19. Only three days after the first.

> Dear Daddy is going to leave me! He has to go on a business trip. He says it will only take a few days, but I shall be so lonely.
> A friend of his will come to stay with me. I don't want a friend of his —I want dear Daddy.
> He leaves tomorrow.
> Dear Diary, I don't want to confide any more—even in you.
> I want to cry.

July 19, leaving tomorrow—make that July 20. That was the day, now Dr. Morris Feldman was sure, that Joel Barrett had been arrested on suspicion of murder.

Where was Tiny? What had happened to her?

2

The telephone's ringing awakened Julio. The blonde beside him stirred, grumbled in her sleep, but did not awaken. He glanced at the luminous dial of his wrist watch: one-seventeen. He swore softly. Why couldn't they leave him alone at this hour? Well, might as well get it over with. He picked up the phone from the bedside table. "Yes?"

"Julio?" A male voice.

"Who is it?"

"Captain Bowden. I'm calling from a phone booth. A dame, a black broad, jumped or was pushed from a window at 259 East 57th Street, Apartment 19M. That's Mame's place, isn't it?"

Julio swore softly. Bowden could be trusted; he was in the book for $2,500 each year. "Used to be until about a month ago. Then it was sublet. The manager, a man named Randall, can give you the man's name."

"Well, there's nobody there now. No dames. No johns. Nothing. Crazy automated lock on the door; we had to break it down. No telephone. No TV. The windows hermetically sealed—how she fell through one I can't figure."

"I'll work on it from my end," Julio said.

"I think you'd better. The heat will be on. The reporters are there now. Remember what happened in Chicago when that dame fell out of the Hancock?"

"Yeah. Thanks," Julio said, and hung up.

He put his feet in slippers and walked out of the bedroom to the den, where there was another phone, a tie line—completely private. He picked it up and listened while it rang a dozen times at the other end. When a guttural voice answered uncertainly, he asked, "What's the matter with you?"

"It's the middle of the night, Julio. Don't you sleep? What do you want?"

"Harry Barratt."

"He's in Zurich. Or was yesterday. I got word of the deposit in the numbered account."

"Then he's on his way back?"

"Probably."

"He could be back."

"Possibly."

"I don't want no 'probably's or 'possibly's. I want facts. Get to our man at the airport."

"At this time of night?"

"Then get back to me. As fast as you can. I'll be waiting for your call." He hung up.

He went over and sprawled on the couch, selected a cigar from the humidor on the coffee table, bit the end off, lighted it and drew deeply. Lucille would never have jumped. She had been pushed through that window. But the window was a one-way job, two heavy plates of glass bonded together. Almost impossible to throw somebody through that. The window at the Hancock wasn't that heavy and they still hadn't figured how that woman had fallen through it on the ninety-second floor.

No mention of Tiny. Somebody had gotten to her; probably Harry. Or had he known that somebody—some third party—was onto him? Was that why he had wanted Lucille in the apartment with the Maiden?

Maybe Lucille had been playing both ends. He doubted it, but you had to consider every angle. Harry could have gotten in the bag with some other dame, told her about his caper—and she could have reported to her higher-up, who was planning a snatch to make Harry pay ransom to get his "daughter" back. If she was his daughter. Maybe Harry was only another dirty old man, like himself.

The telephone rang again.

"Julio?"

"Yes."

"Harry arrived on the eleven-thirty P.M. Swissair flight from Zurich. He went through customs immediately, as usual. He was last seen going to the taxi stand."

Julio took a long, deep drag on his cigar. He was silent for a long time.

"You still there?" asked the voice on the other end.

"Yeah. Shut up, I'm thinking."

"Sure, Julio."

Julio put down the phone and began to pace around his book-lined den, chewing and puffing on his cigar. Then he ground it out in an ashtray and went back to the phone.

"Listen carefully."

"Yes, Julio."

"Hit Harry."

"You want a contract?"

"I said hit him. Our best man. Studs."

"Studs! That's five grand, Julio."

"You want to do it yourself and save money?"

The voice tried to chuckle. "No, Julio. I'll get in touch with Studs."

"Don't 'get in touch with' him. Get him. Right now. If you have to go out in the street to his place and haul him out of the sack. He has to hit Harry before Harry talks. The Feds will be into this, asking interesting questions about why Harry was in Zurich; then when they find out he goes every month, it'll blow his cover and our operation."

"Where will I tell Studs to find Harry?"

"He's in that building—259 East 57th Street—somewhere. He's got to be. At this time of night, there's only one entrance—the front door where the doorman stands. The service entrance is locked and under the doorman's surveillance with closed-circuit TV. The same with the entrance to the garage—the doorman buzzes any latecomer in only after he has recognized him as a tenant on the TV screen.

"Harry has to get out of there sometime, probably with Tiny. Studs should watch that door. He's to hit Harry, leave anyone with him alone. You got a picture of Harry?"

"Yeah."

"A recent one?"

"The one on his passport."

"It'll have to do. Get going!"

Julio went back to the bedroom, threw the covers off the

blonde and slapped her on the fanny until she woke up. He never liked laying a sleeping gash: he wanted a little cooperation.

At 2:50 A.M. that morning, a lean, tanned, handsome man wearing a Cardin suit and carrying expensive luggage registered in the Hotel Grovenor and was shown, at his request, a front suite on a low floor—the third. He tipped the bellman generously and double-locked and bolted the door. Then he opened the suitcase and deftly assembled a .458 Magnum with a tripod and a telescopic sight.

Studs took up his station by the window. Through the sight he could see the screens of the TV monitor, even the color of the doorman's eyes. . . .

3

Dr. Morris Feldman was in Las Vegas. He was standing at the roulette wheel, watching it spin. He had a tall pile of chips in front of him, but he had made no bet. On his right stood a beautiful woman, with long platinum-blond hair down her back, in a sheath gown of silver lamé with a deep décolletage. To his left was a black woman, handsome and elegant, with blood on her face. The croupier was Joel Barrett, in white tie and tails—the Devil!

"Make your bets," Joel said softly.

Eighteen or twenty? That was Morris's choice.

"If I bet eighteen?" he mumbled aloud.

"You might lose," the croupier said.

"If I bet twenty?"

"I might lose," the croupier said.

Morris awoke in a sweat. He remembered the dream vividly, every part of it. And as a psychiatrist, he knew what it meant. Or at least, he thought he did. The important part of knowing other people's minds was not being sure you knew your own.

But another important part was that when you knew you were sure, no one ever knew you were sure but you— making that leap to the pretense of reality that you could thrust upon the patient seductively and make him think it was hers.

Because there was always the problem of *him* and *her*— the gender ambiguity, which our society pretends to ignore. Everyone is male and female.

Christopher Robin, you've lapsed into jargon. Eighteen or twenty, the dream said. Joel is the croupier. Tiny, your patient, stands on your right; the black woman with the bloody face on your left.

"Make your bet!"

Morris sprang out of bed. He had read the dream. Before going to sleep he had assumed that Joel was arrested on July 20, therefore—from the contents of *My Diary*—he was circumstantially suspect of the crime of abducting and sequestering his stepdaughter, Tiny.

But did that mean, what he had dreamed, that he, Morris, might be mistaken, that Joel had been arrested not on the twentieth—but on the eighteenth?

He had to make his bet.

He went into the living room of his apartment, where the papers were piled everywhere. He began to dig in them. His wife had objected to his tendency to collect old newspapers. When he called them "my files," she had countered, "I thought you kept your files in your office." So he did, but these were different files. His files in the office, on his patients, had to do with private worlds. His files here, at home, had to do with the world *out there,* or at least, that other world as journalists saw it.

149

Priscilla had such lovely breasts. The last time he had glimpsed her, she had flaunted them at him. He had had several reactions: to seize her, bury himself in her mammary flurry, penetrate, delve, leave her gasping; or to ignore her last display, go through the door and lock himself out forever; or to use all his knowledge and tell her what he knew as a husband, as well as a psychiatrist: that all that could help her was to go back to the beginning and start over—transmigration of the soul, perhaps.

He had done none of these.

And just because a patient, today, had also had a wife who objected to his tendency to collect old newspapers, he was going to delve into the pile of them as much as he wanted.

He soon found the paper he wanted.

It was the sensational daily.

It was dated July 18.

Its headline on the front page declared: THE DEVIL CHARGED WITH MURDER OF MAIDEN: ON SUSPICION.

Dr. Morris Feldman went to the telephone and dialed the private number Chief Inspector Charles Waverly had given him.

There were clicks, interruptions, curious electronic sounds. Then it rang. And rang. And rang.

4

Chief Inspector Charles Waverly had been born in the Red Hook section of Brooklyn in 1927, the last of seven children. His father was a bartender when working, a steady drinker whether working or not. His mother took in wash and his elder brothers and one sister picked it up and delivered it, carrying the huge bundles on the BMT—which cost a nickel each way—to Flatbush, where Mrs. Waverly's well-off customers lived. By the time Charles was seven he was going for and delivering the laundry himself, because, though strong, he was so thin and little he could go under the turnstiles without the cashier in the booth seeing him, thereby saving the family ten cents subway fare per wash.

Red Hook was not a nice place in which to grow up; to make it you had to be tough. Charles and his brothers were tough. Their father, when sober, was tough. They used to pray for rainy days because when the weather was bad Aloysius Waverly could carry his huge umbrella, furled, to the A & P. Just before he reached the market he would open it and hold it out in the rain so that the outer side of the fabric glistened with raindrops; then he would close it, but not furl it. Inside the store, he would slip cans of beans and peas, jars of peanut butter, jelly and jam, oranges, apples, boxes of cereal, or even sometimes a couple of fish or a bit of ham—though this was harder since there were individual butchers in those days and little open display of meat—cheeses, pickles, catsup, anything he felt he could steal because no one was watching, into the cavernous insides of the giant wet umbrella. Then he would ostentatiously buy a bottle of milk and give the clerk fifteen cents for it and go bravely out into the rain.

When he worked, Aloysius Waverly tended bar at the better restaurants, hotels and clubs of Manhattan; this was before Prohibition. He was an excellent bartender when sober and prided himself on knowing exactly the proper size and shape of glass for every drink. He would become incensed if he saw a fellow worker, or a waiter substituting at the bar, put port in a sherry glass, use a pony for brandy instead of an inhaler, serve a martini in a glass that had not been frosted.

Charles's father was more or less steadily employed at

Manhattan speakeasies until Prohibition was ended, when Charles was six going on seven. "Making liquor legal again was the death of him," Agnes Waverly, Charles's mother, used to sigh. "As long as he knowed it was against the law to drink, and he felt he had to confess his little nips every Saturday—and do the Hail Marys the good priest would make his penance—your father kept to the straight and narrow, more or less."

Aloysius never took the subway to Manhattan when he was working, or on his way back either. He used only the streetcars, riding each one until the conductor came along for his jitney, then pretending to search his pockets for the coin until the exasperated conductor threw him off; repeating the process with the next streetcar that came along— and the next, and the next if necessary—until he reached the Brooklyn Bridge, which he would cross on foot. If the bar, restaurant or, later, speakeasy was in downtown Manhattan—which often it was since Charles's father preferred the City Hall and Wall Street area because he believed the tips were larger there—after leaving the bridge he would walk the rest of the way to work. "It's not that your pap is stingy," his mother would say to young Charles. "It's only that he is prudent with his money."

Prudent or not, there was never enough to go around. Aloysius was also given to betting on horses, "improving the breed," and in turn, each of Charles's older brothers took after him. There were high times and extravagances when one of the "bangtails" came in, but most often morose spirits and too many potatoes in the stew. Even as a boy Charles made up his mind that he would apply himself to his studies and make a mark for himself in the world. It meant many a licking suffered in the yard of the parochial school he attended or along the sidewalks of Red Hook at

the hands of the longshoremen's sons who were his mates
—until Charles learned to keep a rock tied in a sock in his
hip pocket, how to use a knife and where to hit or kick to
disable the biggest boy. After that they left him alone, although they still cat-called at him as he walked the streets
and called him Four-Eyes to his face.

He worked hard at his studies and was accepted at a
selective public high school in the Bronx, to which his
father refused to pay his subway fare each day; his mother
gladly sneaked it to him.

Then one night in Charles's senior year, his oldest
brother, Dickie, whom none of them had seen for months
—though Charles had heard he was running policy for
Owney Madden—came home. There was a honking in the
street and his mother peeped through the lace curtains, to
see Dickie's body thrown from a limousine, which then
sped off. Charles had run with her to the street and had
held her head while she moaned, gasped and retched over
the bullet-ridden carcass that had until recently been her
son. It was then that Charles made up his mind to be a
cop.

He was sitting now in the bathroom in the dark—cold,
miserable, as angry as ever with the world as it had been
then and still was (no, it was worse, worse!). Unable to
sleep, he had turned down the bell of the telephone, something a good cop should never do, and hidden himself in
the bathroom.

Even so, he could hear it ringing again. Well, if he hadn't
done this duty by now, he probably wouldn't, bound
though he was. He had best attend to his other, overween-
ing duty. He pulled up his pajama pants, opened the door
and fumbled his way in the dark to the phone, hoping to
keep from waking his wife, Maggie.

It was that tarnal idiot of a psychiatrist, a gossoon if ever there was one.

But he said he had found valuable evidence about the Maiden's kidnapping. A diary.

"I'll meet you at my office in half an hour," Chief Inspector Charles Waverly said.

5

Dr. Morris Feldman, the nut doctor, found Tigger in his element at his office in Centre Street early that muggy July morning. He sat behind his solid oak desk, feet upon it, shoes off, unshaven, flanked, on the dun-colored wall behind him, by the framed autographed photographs of police commissioners under whom he had served. The current commissioner was not represented. The door to his private bathroom stood open. He waved Morris to a chair beside his desk and noted his glance toward the open door.

"You're an M.D., doc?"

"Yes, though I practice as a psychiatrist."

"But you went through medical school, right?"

"That I did."

"What does it mean when you feel you have to go, but it just won't come?"

"Probably nothing."

"What do you mean—probably nothing?"

"Just that. Most constipation is the result only of nervous tension. If it persists—"

"Ever since I jailed the magician."

"You mean Joel?"

"Yeah."

"That was July eighteenth."

"Yeah."

"Not long enough to worry about. Tell me, do you often have these symptoms when a case is worrying you?"

"Yeah. Almost always."

"Martin Luther decided to defy the Pope when he was constipated."

"But I'm a Catholic. I don't go to confession every week, but I'm a Catholic."

"It doesn't matter. The same principle applies."

"What principle?" the chief inspector asked.

"Nervous tension."

"What do you mean by that? Tell me."

"The gut is a spastic instrument. Think of it as a long, corrugated tube. It expands and contracts—normally—according to the contents that are passing through it. Normally we have no control over it."

"We just eat, and then the stuff comes out."

"Yes. But when we are tense, when we are upset emotionally, this tension causes the colon to contract when it should be emollient; when it should be easing the passage of the fecal matter, it blocks it."

"So all I have to do is take a tranquilizer and it will be all right?"

"I'd recommend against a tranquilizer at this time. But I wouldn't worry," Morris advised.

"Why no tranquilizer? I thought all you shrinks were for them?"

"Some are."

"You're not?"

"Not in your case."

"You think I'm just going to have to be tough shit until I figure this thing out?"

"Yes."

"You know, even though you're a psychiatrist, you're a good doc."

"Thank you."

"I knew I threw a lot of things at you. But I had to."

"I know. And I also know you're an old fraud."

"Not so old, you young gossoon—I'll only be fifty my next birthday."

"What's a gossoon?"

"Just like a shrink—you want me to tell you everything. Now, where's this diary, or whatever you call it, that you called me down here practically in the middle of the night for?"

Morris opened his briefcase and gave Chief Inspector Waverly Tiny's diary, which he had picked up from the sidewalk on East Fifty-seventh Street.

Waverly read it rapidly, even greedily, then placed it carefully on his desk.

"Where did you say you found this?"

"On East Fifty-seventh Street, within half a block of the building Tiny Barrett used to live in with her father."

"Any other special circumstances?"

"Yes, there was a commotion in the street."

"Where?"

"About a block—no, I'd say a half block, farther east."

"What did you do?"

"I took a cab. And the cabby told me what had happened. A woman, a young black woman, had fallen to the street in front of Tiny's building. He said she was dead."

Inspector Waverly opened the right-hand drawer of his desk and picked up the phone. He dialed it. "Get me Captain Bowden. I don't care where the hell he is—get him." He thrust the phone back in the drawer and slammed it shut. He smiled benignly at Dr. Morris Feldman.

"Now, if you'll excuse me, I think I'll go and relieve myself."

He went into his private bathroom and slammed the door.

Chief Inspector Waverly came back a few minutes later, obviously relaxed. He sank down in his executive-type upholstered chair and for the first time in Morris's experience with him smiled broadly. Only briefly, however, his lips returning to their usual dour expression almost at once, as if he remembered himself. Then he bent over and jerked open the right-hand drawer of his desk, grabbed the concealed phone and dialed it. "Where's Bowden? What do you mean—no telephone? Get to him—I don't care how. Send a scout car, dummy! Tell him I want to speak to him at once!"

Waverly leaned back in his chair and regarded Morris. "You're not a Catholic?"

"No. I was born a Jew."

"Martin Luther—he was a Catholic once."

"Once. But then he founded Protestantism."

"Did he believe in the Devil?"

"I'm no theologian, but yes, I think he did."

"Do you?"

"Here I'm on firmer ground, Inspector. Personally, no, I do not believe in the Devil—as Satan, as Beelzebub, as a fallen angel, an adversary of God who wrestles with him for men's souls. However, as long as any of my patients do so believe, then in order to care for them, to identify with their problems, to have insight into their emotions and complexes—yes, I do."

"Do you think Joel Barrett is the Devil, or a personification of him?"

"No, I do not. But I do think it likely that the person who has abducted his daughter Tiny may well believe him to be

157

—and that this person is trying to free her from what he considers her stepfather's 'malevolent influence.' "

"This sociopath?"

"Yes."

"You get this from the diary?" Waverly rapped the book with the back of his hand.

"The passages in the diary only confirm suspicions I've had before. They are a cry for help, obviously written to appease the irrational, if narrowly moralistic, demands of her captor. Even so, she has managed to cram enough between the lines to inform us of the hellish imprisonment she must be going through."

"Hmm. How did it happen to be on East Fifty-seventh Street?"

"I've thought a lot about that. Could her captor have dropped it by mistake?"

"Possibly. You keep saying 'her captor,' without referring specifically to sex. Does this mean you think whoever abducted her might be a woman?"

"It's not to be ruled out, is it?"

"Hmm. And a young woman was found dead in the street, having been pushed or having jumped from a high place, close to where you found the diary."

He grabbed at the drawer again, had seized the phone, when it began to ring. "Bowden?"

Morris heard loud, excited speech on the wire, even from where he sat.

"Well, why the hell didn't you get in touch with me? You did try—well, you could've tried the office. Tell me about it; I'll listen."

And Waverly did listen, taking notes on his scratch pad. "Well, keep on with the investigation. I'll be up there shortly."

He slammed down the phone, only to dial it again immediately. "All right. Get this straight for once. We're holding two men. The name is Joel Barrett for the first one. That's right, the magician. He's being held on suspicion of murder. No two *r*'s, an *e,* two *t*'s—Barrett. Now you got it right.

"The second is Nick Cavolla. That's right. He's being held as a material witness. Both in the disappearance of Sheila Barrett. That's right—the Maiden.

"I want them both released in my recognizance and brought to my office. At once. What? Wake them up. Wake up the property clerk too. Don't argue, do it!"

Waverly cradled the receiver violently and glowered at Morris.

"We're going to need all the help we can get."

8

THE DEVIL AND
THE MAIDEN

Tigger, alias Chief Inspector Charles Waverly, seemed more at ease now than Morris Feldman had ever seen him. The eyes were still brown buttons, but there was a light in them; the wispy mustache still resembled the bedraggled whiskers of a child's stuffed animal, but they appeared to have some character, some bristle. Possibly what he had needed all along was a complete evacuation?

He even offered Morris a cigar, which, after the psychiatrist refused, he took for himself, biting off the end and lighting slowly and carefully with a kitchen match. Then he waved his hand around his office. "I've got everything here—police teletype, constant two-way communication with each and every precinct, and through the precinct with any squad car, daily reports from every precinct captain, every chief of detectives, even the confidential squads. And yet this time, an amateur has come in and told me how to run my operation."

"If I've been of help—"

"We'll see. I've doubts yet. You don't come up from pounding the pavement in the days when there was no fancy-spansy police academy, or university classes with professors to teach young men and women how to become undercover agents, without knowing that most cases are solved by jackass labor and tips from stool pigeons.

"But we've had more than sixty people on this job day and night. And we've come up with too little—I won't say nothing, but too damn little."

"What have you come up with? May I ask?" Morris said.

"Sure. That's why I'm talking to you. You haven't heard any of this before, and now you deserve to know. Maybe you can make more of it than we have, than I have."

He paused and Morris knew better than to interrupt.

Then, after several long and thoughtful puffs on his cigar, Waverly continued. "Early in the morning of June 12, Sheila Barrett was last seen by the bartender Nick Cavolla in his bed and in his apartment. The night doorman at 259 East 57th Street left his post to go home after the day man came on duty. That was a few minutes after seven A.M.—the day man can't say for sure, though he knows he was a little late.

"The night doorman followed his usual habit. He walked toward the Lexington Avenue subway to go home to the Bronx. It was a warm morning and the day man went out on the street and saw him begin to cross to Lexington Avenue, then he went back inside to his post. That was the last he ever saw of him."

"What happened to him?" Morris had to ask.

"He was run over by a Lexington Avenue express at the Fifty-ninth Street station. That early in the morning, there were apparently no witnesses; the motorman didn't see how it happened. 'Fell or was pushed,' the medical examiner's report said."

"You think it was murder?"

"We have yet to rule out the possibility—the probability, from what I have learned tonight."

"But why kill an old man?"

"Because he knew something—or saw someone with someone."

"You have thought all along it was Joel—that's why you had him arrested and held in such high bail he hasn't yet been able to raise it?"

"I would have to say yes—and for another reason too."

"What's that?"

"For his own protection."

"Are you saying that whoever has done this might have killed Joel?"

"Yes. Exactly."

"Then why didn't you tell him as much?" Morris asked.

"Because on the evidence, he was our leading suspect."

"Evidence. What evidence?"

"Let's begin with yours, doctor. You are the one who told me he came to you and said that his stepdaughter had awakened in what she thought to be a television stage set of his own devising—without her clothes, but with a closet-ful of childish garments, some of which she had to put on to come back home. He told you she had accused him of this plot against her, and that she had packed her clothes and left him—'left the act'—because of it."

"That is so. But why did this lead you to believe Joel Barrett was the one most likely to have abducted his step-daughter?"

"Your profile, doctor. 'The man we are seeking is a sociopath who is driven to test the barriers of society.' Here we have a man who makes his living as a magician impersonating the Devil and apparently committing sadistic acts against a young woman who impersonates the Maiden—who also happens to be his own stepdaughter, or so he professes. And you yourself told me that this same man expressed to you desires he considered to be incestuous."

162

"But even so, this is all circumstantial. There are no witnesses."

"That is what has made this case so difficult. It is all circumstantial. A young woman, a capable and talented performer on TV, vanishes under conditions that at first seemed to be incredibly like her own television performances."

"So you thought it was a publicity act of Joel Barrett's that had possibly misfired?"

"Didn't you? Wasn't that strongly in your mind when I first talked with you?" Waverly asked.

"But that was in June. Now we're near the end of July. There is the diary I found tonight near her home, which I take to mean she is still being kept captive and is seeking help—and Joel has been in prison since July eighteenth. But the contents of the diary show that Tiny was still in the presence of and held captive by her abductor as late as July twentieth, the day before yesterday."

"Which is why I have had Joel released on my recognizance. The evidence—still all circumstantial, Dr. Feldman —seems now to absolve him of the actual kidnapping or incarceration."

"But then why did you hold Nick Cavolla as a material witness?"

"He was the last man to have seen her alive. He was her lover. Both, from the point of view of day-in-day-out police procedure, are highly suspicious circumstances. Nine out of ten times in a disappearance, the last man to see a young woman alive who was also her lover is also her murderer.

"But beyond that, a fact that led us to believe Mr. Cavolla is not implicated, she volunteered to him a description of the apartment to which she had first been abducted—and from which she escaped to return to her stepfather and then flee to Mr. Cavolla—an apartment decorated all in white, with no possibility of communication with the outside world, in which she was made to play the part of the daughter of her abductor. It fits with what her stepfather said she told him when she accused him of tricking her onto a 'television set'; it fits with what she told you about needing to leave the act and fearing to—"

"You thought Nick might have abducted her?" the psychiatrist asked.

"Possibly. But he was the only one with a description of the place where she had been taken."

"So why arrest him?"

"He is important—an important witness, if nothing else, whom the actual perpetrator, if it isn't himself, would like to see removed."

"For his own good, then." Morris sighed.

"Yes, if you wish."

"So the two men who might help you most, the two men most motivated to help you, you've had behind bars. In the meantime, have you found the apartment?"

"Yes, I think we may have."

"What! If you know where she is, why aren't we there now? Why hasn't she been rescued?"

"We have in fact located and are in possession of this— uh—residence, and Sheila Barrett is not there."

"Then where the hell is she?" Morris asked.

Chief Inspector Waverly was fiddling with his desk-drawer intercom. He spoke into it. "Yes. They're both there? And Captain Bowden? Send him in first." Waverly glowered at Morris. All his equanimity had gone.

"You might as well sit here and listen to this, doctor. And see what I have to deal with. . . ."

Waverly sounded like a little boy who had been promised cookies and milk before going to bed and whose mother had forgotten.

But don't we all sound that way sometimes, Morris wondered. Even if we have become chief inspectors?

2

Captain Benson Bowden came into the room. Exuding the air of the perpetual veteran, he wore his uniform, with all its brass, with ease. He wore his stature—at least six foot three inches—equally casually. His broad shoulders and taut waist, his large hands with long fingers, all were at the alert and simultaneously relaxed. It was the mustache that gave him away—heavy, bristly, just barely kempt.

"You wanted to see me?" he asked the inspector.

"Yes."

Bowden continued standing. Chief Inspector Waverly was Tigger again, the stuffed pussycat that could strike with no warning.

"You called me in the night?"

"Yes; I thought it was necessary."

"Well, this dame that I told you jumped—"

"Yes?"

"She jumped from that building you asked me to keep under surveillance," Bowden said.

"Yes. But I received your phone call at three A.M., just as I was leaving to come down here. I knew already about the suicide."

"That hasn't as yet been determined."

"What?"

"That she was a suicide."

"What else?"

"She could have fallen. Or she could've been pushed," Bowden said.

"How?"

"That we don't know yet."

"Why not?"

"Jesus, Inspector—it's only five in the morning now. Give us a little time."

"Have you identified the body?"

"No."

"Why not?"

"Look, Inspector, be reasonable. A dame jumps or, if you want, was pushed or fell from the nineteenth story of an apartment building on East Fifty-seventh Street. Right? We get the call about one-thirty A.M. We're there at once—I mean at once. All equipment before two. It's on the records."

"But you didn't get through to me until nearly three—just before I was leaving the apartment."

"There's no phone in the place. I had to go out on the street. I was busy."

"What place?"

"The apartment she fell from—or jumped, or was pushed."

"Describe it to me."

"It's all in white. No lock on the door—only some kind of crazy slot. No radio. No TV. But luxury all the way. The real McCoy."

"What's the number?"

"You mean of the apartment?"

"Yes."

"It was 19M."

"That was Mame's place, wasn't it?"

"Yes. But Mame's place didn't look like this."

"You've been in Mame's place?"

"I'm the captain of the precinct."

"Did you find out who rents 19M?"

"It's a sublet. A man named Harry Barratt."

"Not Joel Barrett?"

"No, Harry."

"How is the last name spelled?"

"*B-a*-double *r-a*-double *t.*"

"How long is his lease?"

"It's a sublease."

"How long?"

"Indeterminate."

"Who is the lessor? No, don't bother answering. I know. As soon as you leave this office, call Julio Bacigaluppi on an outside phone. Tell him I want to see him in an hour in my office."

"Julio?"

"Yes, *Julio.* Now get out."

As soon as Captain Bowden slammed the door, Tigger turned to Morris. "He's not a bad kid. Korean war veteran. Went right up to the Yalu River with MacArthur. Then he joined the force. Hero cop. Shot seven men dead in five attempted holdups in Harlem and Bedford-Stuyvesant. Twice in plain clothes. Went to college at night. Now he heads up the lushest precinct in town and is into this Julio. This may bust him. But I was kind to him."

"You were kind to him?" Morris asked.

"I could have told him you are a psychiatrist."

He activated his intercom.

"Tell Mr. Cavolla to come in."

3

Nick Cavolla struck Morris as a rapier of a man. He came into Chief Inspector Waverly's office like a riposte and was at his desk in what appeared to be a single bound. He stood at the point of a lunge, his hands flat on the desktop. "You wanted to see me?"

"Yes. I called for you."

"It's about time."

Again Dr. Feldman observed a different attitude, a different stance, in Chief Inspector Waverly. He stood. He put *his* hands down flat on *his* side of the desk. He leaned ever so slightly toward the bartender who had been Tiny's first lover.

"You have any complaints?" Waverly asked.

"I'm going to sue the city for false arrest," Nick said.

"Your lawyer suggested that?"

"No, but I told him I'm going to anyway. What kind of crap are you trying to make me eat? I meet a young woman. She's in trouble. Worried. I take her home to dinner. She leaves. She comes back later with her things and a weird story about her stepfather trying to force her into a television act she doesn't want to appear in—at least I think that was what she was trying to say. So I say she can shack up with me. So we go to bed. Big deal! Then I wake up and she's gone. And the next thing I know, I'm under arrest as a material witness. Why?"

"As I'm sure your lawyer must have explained to you, you were the last to see her alive."

"You think she's dead?"

"I really don't know."

"You mean the poor kid may have been murdered?" Nick paled.

"Why don't you sit down, Mr. Cavolla?"

Nick sat, but first he looked around the office. Pointing to Morris, he said, "Who's he?"

"Dr. Morris Feldman."

"What's he doing here?"

"He is Sheila Barrett's psychiatrist."

"She told me about him. Why isn't *he* under arrest?"

"Because in my judgment, he is not under suspicion, and his life is not in danger."

"You think that he—whoever has done this—might have been out to kill me?"

"You were the last to see her. You are the one to whom she described the apartment."

"Is that so important?"

"Pivotal. You could, if you would, repeat again—as you remember it, as close to Tiny's actual words as you can come—her description of the apartment, or 'television set,' as she called it, in which she had been held captive."

"That tall guy with the mustache and the gestures who was sitting out there with me. Is he the Devil—her stepfather?" Nick asked.

"He is Joel Barrett."

"Then why aren't you asking *him* questions?"

"I am going to be asking him questions in just a little while."

"But I gave this all to you before," Nick said.

"Do you want to help Tiny?"

"Of course. You mean I may have left something out before?"

"Exactly."

"Well, I'll try. You see, she had come to me that night. When I woke up and saw she'd gone, I thought, 'one of those things.' "

"That was the night of June tenth."

"Yes. Then she came back the next day—just before I was about to go off work."

"That's June eleventh?"

"Yes. You got this all down before."

"Yes."

"But you want to see if you can catch me in any discrepancies?"

Waverly merely said, "And what happened?"

"She arrived with her suitcase. I took her home."

"Why did she say she was there?"

"I asked her if she had walked out on Joel. She said she had. I asked why. She wouldn't say. If I remember correctly, she said, 'Not now, maybe later.' She said he had played a dirty trick on her. She wouldn't tell me what it was. But she wanted me to know that something real had happened—that she wasn't being hysterical, as she said her psychiatrist thought she might be." Morris saw that Nick was careful not to look at him.

Tigger *was* looking at him. "You thought she might have been hysterical?"

"Yes. And I told her so. An error in judgment, in view of later events."

"Thank you, Dr. Feldman," Tigger said.

"She said her psychiatrist had told her that she had a tendency to act out her hidden resentments," Nick said.

"Did you say that?" Tigger asked.

"Yes. I still believe it to be so," Morris replied. And what about you, you old fraud?

"What did you do then?" the chief inspector asked Nick.

"I gave her a drink. She needed a friend."

"How many?"

"Three, I think."

"What kind of drink?"

"Margaritas."

"Did she get intoxicated?"

"A little. Which I thought, at that point, was what was prescribed. Then I fixed her a steak, baked potato. She ate it all."

"And then you laid her?"

"No. We talked."

"What did you talk about?"

"Personal things—personal to her. The first thing she remembered. Lying in a hospital bed scared to death. But she said someone was holding her hand. Someone was saying that she knew it hurt, Patricia, but it would be all right, she would be all better."

"Patricia? Someone called her not Sheila, but Patricia?"

"Yes. She said that was her real name. But she was so small they called her Tiny. Then later, when she became tall, they still called her Tiny—I guess the way as kids we used to call a skinny guy Fats."

"What else did she say about her background?"

"She told me about her stepfather, Joel—the guy she had just run away from. How her real father had deserted her mother, how her mother had got a job singing with a band that was on tour, how she had fallen sick and her mother had stayed with her and when her fever ran high, taken her to a hospital."

"And then?"

"This guy Joel—she says he's her stepfather—came on the scene. Her mother was out of money, so I take it she shacked up with Joel. Anyway, he was a magician, a 'star act,' I remember Tiny said. He paid her hospital bills, took care of them, made her mother part of the act. Tiny, when she grew older and recovered from the polio—that's why she was in the hospital—became his assistant, after her mother died in a car smash." Nick grimaced. "I still don't know why you had to hear all that again."

Tigger offered him a cigar, which Nick refused.

"Did she talk about the act, about how she had persuaded her stepfather to change it?" Waverly asked.

"Yeah. I told you that. She became aware that audiences don't care for what she called 'straight magic' any more—

171

sawing a woman in half, making an elephant disappear. It's got to be gruesome. They want to see her put in the Iron Maiden, knowing that she'll come out bloody but alive. But maybe the next time . . ."

Chief Inspector Charles Waverly focused his eyes on Dr. Morris Feldman.

Morris nodded. Somehow the core of the case was in what had just been said. But, he was now sure, it didn't lie with Joel. "Not Joel," he said softly.

"But who?" Waverly asked.

"I don't know," Morris said. "There must be some factor we are missing, some other person who is involved that we don't know about."

Tigger snorted.

Nick was talking again. "After she had left me in the middle of the night, she went back to the place where she lived—that apartment building. She remembered talking with the doorman, then getting into the elevator. Then she remembered nothing until she had awakened that afternoon, a little more than an hour before she came into my bar."

"Where was she?"

"She didn't know. She awoke on a white, heart-shaped bed. She was wearing a white nightgown she had never seen before, with a slip underneath. She couldn't find any of her own clothes.

"She started to explore the apartment. It was all white— the carpeting, the walls, the furniture. There were three other bedrooms, two unoccupied. She said the other one had Joel's things in it. Her closet was filled with old-fashioned clothes."

Morris broke in. "How did she know they were Joel's things?"

"His white dress suit, I suppose. The one he wears on TV."

"You suppose?" Waverly asked. "Did Tiny say so?"

"I don't know. It's hard to say. I remember that she said she had explored the apartment. There was no telephone. No knob on the door. She felt trapped.

"Then she went to the closet in the other occupied bedroom and she said, if I remember right, 'All his things were there—even a white suit in the closet, the sort of thing they wear now instead of a full-dress suit, with white satin lapels.' She found the card there—the one that would open the knobless door. There was a slit, see, on the inside of the door, and you put the card in there, like a credit card, which takes the place of a key."

"So then what did she do?"

"She dressed herself in one of those crazy, old-fashioned outfits he had left for her, put the card in the slot, opened the door, went home—and gave him hell. She told him she was leaving the act, packed her bag, slammed out of there with her bag, came to me, and I took her to my place."

"She spent the night with you—the night of June eleventh–twelfth?"

"I awoke about dawn to find her gone."

"And she hasn't been seen since?"

"You know that, Inspector, as well as I do. Why don't you find that all-white apartment with the white, heart-shaped bed?"

"I think we have," said Chief Inspector Waverly.

4

Tiny was beginning to feel, if not comfortable, *almost* without discomfort in the Iron Maiden. She knew she mustn't move, and she hadn't. "Think of a candle burning bright, think of a candle against the night. Only there is no candle, and it is not burning bright, it is not burning at all. It has no wick. It has no light. But think of that candle burning bright." That was what Uncle Eddie had told her she must do—and she was doing it.

She was bleeding. She was bleeding. She could feel the warmth of her own blood. Later it would be cold, clammy. But as long as it was warm, as long as she could see the candle, the candle burning bright against the night, a candle that didn't exist, with no wick or light, as long as she could see that candle, she would be all right—even in the Iron Maiden.

Her pulse must be slow, shallow, and *even*. She must not become lethargic as she walked the tightrope between life and death. Calm. She must stay calm. "A quiver of a muscle," Uncle Eddie had said, "can betray you." But that was when he was teaching her the act, teaching her how to stay for prolonged periods within the Iron Maiden. But Uncle Eddie wasn't here now. Joel wasn't here now. No one was here now. Unless Harry was—Harry, who had locked her into this devilish device.

She had to keep from being lethargic. It was important that her pulse be slowed, that her breathing become shallow while staying regular. But she had to keep the oxygen/ nitrogen content in her blood stable. She had to think, remember, a little.

Tiny remembered putting on once again the middy blouse, the knickers, the Mary Janes, that Harry felt suitable. She had walked past the gaping hole of the window from which her friend Lucille had been thrown. She had allowed Harry's slight pressure upon her back as he had inserted the card in the slot and opened the door. She had shuffled behind him to the elevator.

He hadn't pressed down, but up!

They had gone up one floor, along the short hall, then up the stairs to the penthouse!

He had opened the door to *her* home with his key. He had shown her into her own home! Joel wasn't there. Harry had taken over the penthouse!

She could feel her pulse quickening, feel the sharp caress of the Iron Maiden lacerating her flesh. . . .

"Think of a candle burning bright, think of a candle against the night. . . ."

5

Chief Inspector Waverly's telephone rang. He jerked open the drawer and pulled out the handset in exasperation, as if it were a live thing that was purposely exasperating him.

"Yes? Well, send him in." He looked at Nick and Morris. "Julio Bacigaluppi. You may as well stay and hear what he has to say."

The psychiatrist and the bartender glanced at each other. According to the newspapers, Julio Bacigaluppi had taken over control of the syndicate from Gallo and Colombo. Now he was appearing in Waverly's office in connection with the disappearance of Tiny?

He was a small man, with thinning gray hair. He wore a red sports jacket, white flannel slacks, white patent-leather shoes with gold buckles. "You wanted to see me so early in the morning? It must be important."

"Thank you for coming down, Julio," Chief Inspector Waverly said. Morris noted his deferential tone.

"I'm always obliged to cooperate with you, Charles. Just remember, you get to be king, I want to be treasurer." Julio had sat in the remaining chair, his feet crossed delicately at the ankles.

"A woman jumped, or was thrown, from a window at 259 East 57th Street early this morning. A young black woman. Dressed in a maid's uniform. Do you know anything about it?"

"Her name is Lucille Belleville. An interior decorator. She worked for me from time to time." He shook his head sadly. "A brilliant young woman."

"When did you see her last?"

"Day before yesterday. In my office. We talked about a business matter she wanted my advice on."

"A business matter?"

"A mutual friend wanted to hire her at a very high rate of pay to work a few days as the French maid to his girlfriend. I suppose there was a kick in it for him somewhere."

"Miss Belleville was a maid?"

"No, no. I told you—an interior decorator."

"She designed and furnished your cathouses for you?" Julio shrugged. "If you want to put it that way, yes."

"What did you advise her day before yesterday?"

"Take the money. Be a maid for a little while. I was mistaken."

"What do you think happened?" Waverly inquired.

"Now you're asking me to do your work for you."

"But you must have some idea."

"None."

"You are the lessee, and sublessor, of apartment 19M at 259 East 57th Street?"

"Yes."

"That was Mame's place until just recently?"

"People called it that."

"Then Mame was out, and a Harry Barratt moved in."

"An old friend," Julio said.

"He had the apartment completely remodeled?"

"Yes. He asked me to recommend somebody. I recommended Lucille Belleville."

"She took care of the whole thing—even to the computerized door?"

"That's right."

"Then he killed her because she knew too much?"

"That could be. Then again, that couldn't be. Charles, I don't know."

"Who is Harry Barratt?"

"An old friend, as I said before."

"He works for you?"

"He worked for me once, in a minor way."

"Why should you sublease 19M—a going business proposition?"

"Money."

"Harry has money?"

"Yes."

"Where did he get it?"

"It's not my business to ask old friends where they got their money, unless I think they're stealing from me."

"Harry isn't stealing from you?"

"No."

"Where do you think he gets his money?"

"Harry travels a lot."

"Cocaine?"

Julio shrugged. "Could be. Couldn't be. It's none of my business."

"Where is he now?"

"In New York."

"But where?"

"You've tried Apartment 19M?"

"There are police all over the place. I'm going there myself shortly."

"You want me to tell you about Harry Barratt?"

"Why the hell do you think I asked you to come down here?"

"So all right. Charles, sometimes I think you get your jollies from yelling at people. It's not nice. And it don't work. People like you and me, people with real power, we can find out more by being polite. Not that I resent it, Charles, don't misunderstand me."

"So tell me about Harry Barratt."

"Do you remember about twenty-two years ago there was a man, an insurance collector, who left his apartment in the morning, kissed his wife and child—he was worried because the child had a fever—and never saw either of them again?"

"How could I remember that?" Waverly jumped up from his desk and began to pace. "It happens all the time. How could I remember that?"

"I'm not saying you should, Charles—but that man was Harry Barratt. He has been looking for that lost child ever since. Now he thinks he has found her. He thinks she has been corrupted."

"Corrupted?"

"He doesn't approve of her show on television with the man who calls himself the Devil. He asked me to sublease him an apartment, and find someone who could decorate it and make it secure. I did. It was a good business proposition."

"But why did he have to kill her?"

"Charles, I don't know that he did."

"And his last name is the same as the girl's—Barrett?"

"No, it's spelled differently: *B-a-r-r-a-t-t.*"

"Do *you* think the Maiden is his daughter?"

"I don't know. Tell me, Charles, didn't I see the Devil outside in your waiting room?"

"Yes, you did."

"Why don't you ask *him* in?"

6

"I don't understand why you aren't dead," Harry said to her after he opened the Iron Maiden.

"Do you want me dead?" Tiny asked as she staggered into his arms.

"No, I want you cleansed of all evil!"

"Right now, I'm a little . . . a little faint."

Tenderly, he carried her into the bathroom. He drew a bathtubful of warm water and bathed her. "How could you survive *that?*" he wondered.

Tiny giggled. It felt nice to have someone lave her with a washcloth, even Harry. "It's all in knowing how." She laughed again. "Are you disappointed?"

"That you're not dead?"

"Yes."

"No, I'm relieved."

"Then you really, truly, didn't want me dead."

"I only want you cleansed of all evil," Harry said.

"Even if it kills me?"

"If it kills you, then you are evil. Then I have stamped out the evil in you."

"So now on to the rack?" Tiny asked.

"Yes. How else can I be sure?"

7

A tall, lank, graceful man strode into Inspector Waverly's office. Joel Barrett had somehow managed to keep himself fastidiously dressed in a white double-breasted suit with white satin lapels during his days in the detention pen. He came through the door, he *entered*, he bestowed upon all of them his *presence*. Morris noted his own use of the word, and once again wondered about Tiny's use of it in his consulting room so long ago, as it now seemed. Was the "presence" she had referred to then a composite, an amalgam of both Harry and Joel?

Before Inspector Waverly could speak to him, Joel was at his desk and then beside him. Waverly began to rise in protest, but the magician restrained him lightly with his left hand upon his shoulder. Then his right hand plucked at Waverly's outer breast pocket, hesitated, began to pull. From that pocket he withdrew a scarlet bandanna, a bright yellow one, and an American flag, which he waved above the inspector's head.

"You see, ladies and gentlemen, it is all illusion," Joel said.

"What the hell do you mean by that?" Waverly said.

"Simply that there is no such thing as magic—alas, only the illusion of magic."

"Look, Mr. Barrett, I had you arrested on suspicion of murder because everything pointed to you being implicated in your stepdaughter's disappearance."

"You were suffering from an illusion," Joel said.

"Maybe. Developments have occurred that indicate I might have been mistaken. But on the other hand, if I hadn't taken you into custody, you might have suffered harm. Do you realize that?"

"It's possible. But I'd have preferred to be outside, helping you actively."

"You can do that, here and now, by answering some questions."

"Very well."

"Is the young woman who was part of your act on TV until just recently, who was billed as the Maiden but known to her friends and associates as Tiny—is she actually your stepdaughter?"

"I adopted her legally, yes."

"You have the adoption papers?"

"They are in Tiny's possession, probably in one of her bureau drawers in the penthouse."

"When did the adoption papers go through?"

"It took quite a while. In the summer of 1950."

"You're lying to me, Mr. Barrett."

"Yes. I did have false adoption papers drawn—to please Sally."

"Sally?"

"My wife, Sally. Tiny's mother. She kept wanting me to adopt Sheila formally."

"Why didn't you?"

"Legal complications."

"What do you mean?"

"I had never been divorced from my first wife, although I had married Sally."

"So you're a bigamist."

"Marriage is an illusion too, which only works as long as you both believe in it."

"You keep referring to your—the Maiden's mother as Sally?"

"That was her stage name when I first met her in Des Moines. I was playing the theater there; she had been with a band that had been there the previous week, before her baby fell sick. She was broke and worried about taking care of the hospital expenses."

"So you began a relationship with her, and picked up her kid's bills?"

"A relationship that lasted until Muriel's untimely death," Joel said.

"Muriel? Now Sally is Muriel?"

Julio had jumped to his feet. "Muriel! Muriel! That's the name of Harry's wife, the one who ran away from him, taking his baby, who he's been looking for ever since!"

Joel turned and stared at Julio. "Who is this man?"

"A witness," Waverly said. He motioned to Julio to be quiet. "Tell me, Mr. Barrett, is your name really Barrett?"

"It has been my stage name for nearly twenty-five years."

"What name did you use before that?"

"White. Joel White."

"Why did you change it?"

"Muriel and I—Sally—were starting out on a new act together. She said White was too common a name. She suggested Barratt, with two *a*'s. I agreed but changed it to Barrett, with an *a* and an *e*. I thought it was easier to remember that spelling."

The chief inspector sank back in his chair, his palm to his forehead. "What will dames think of next!" he cried.

"May I ask you a question, Inspector?" Joel asked quietly.

"You might as well."

"Where is Tiny?"

"I wish I knew. We have found the apartment where she was being held, but she is no longer there."

"Where was it?"

"In your building, two floors below you, 19M."

"Why hadn't you looked there before?"

"I can't go into apartments without search warrants, and I had no reason to suspect that one."

Joel was very angry, but despite the intensity of his response he contained his rage, although he did lean his weight upon the chief inspector's desk. "After all your bumbling, may *I* start looking for Tiny now?"

"You might as well. But call in here at this office or the precinct every day."

Joel rushed out the door, slamming it. Waverly chewed on his cigar, then nodded to Morris. "Don't worry. I have a tail on him. He just may be able to lead us to her."

8

Joel hailed the first cab he saw and gave his East Fifty-seventh Street address. Shoving a bill at the cabby, he jumped out before the vehicle had pulled to the curb. Joel rushed past the doorman to the elevator and took it to the top floor and then bounded up the stairs to the penthouse.

The front door was unlocked, ajar.

The lights were on in the living room. The Iron Maiden had been knocked over, the rack torn apart. Everything was in disorder. Calling her name, Joel ran to Tiny's bedroom. She was not there. Her clothes were all missing from the closet, though a few underthings and a pair of panty hose were strewn on the floor.

He went into the bathroom. Scrawled in lipstick on the mirror of the medicine cabinet were the words: HE IS MY FATHER AND HE HAS TAKEN ME TO HELL!

The only thing Joel could do was to phone Chief Inspector Waverly.

After Waverly had charged out of his office on the way to the penthouse, followed by his retinue, Julio went down the hall to a phone booth. He dialed the number Studs had given him.

"Hello."

"Studs?"

"Yeah."

"You let him go."

"I tell you it's impossible, Julio. Unless he was the guy in the Devil costume with a chick pretending to be Mary Pickford on his arm."

EPILOGUE

From the *New York Times:*

MONUMENTAL LINCOLN TUNNEL TIE-UP

Thousands of motorists and truckers were stalled for more than an hour shortly before noon yesterday when a car-truck collision, explosion and fire clogged one of the westbound tubes of the Lincoln Tunnel. The tie-up occurred when a private car rammed the rear end of a trailer truck loaded with high-octane gasoline. The truckdriver escaped unscathed but the driver of the car and his passenger burned to death before they could be extricated by Port Authority Police. They are as yet unidentified.

The *New York Post* in its last edition that same day repeated approximately the same account of the incident, but its headline revealed a further fact:

MAIDEN DIES IN FLAMING CRASH!

WAS THAT THE DEVIL WITH HER?

"You can never leave someone about whom your feelings are ambivalent."